MAD HATTER'S HOLIDAY

PETER LOVESEY

MAD HATTER'S HOLIDAY

First published in Great Britain in 1973.
This edition published in 2009 by

Soho Press, Inc.
853 Broadway
New York, NY 10003

Library of Congress Cataloging-in-Publication Data

Lovesey, Peter.
Mad hatter's holiday / Peter Lovesey.
p. cm.
ISBN 978-1-56947-560-7 (pbk.)
1. Cribb, Sergeant (Fictitious character)—Fiction. 2. Police—England—
Brighton—Fiction. 3. Brighton (England)—Fiction. I. Title.
PR6062.O86M3 2009
823'.914—dc22
2008042637

10 9 8 7 6 5 4 3 2 1

Mad hatter's holiday

CHAPTER 1

BRIGHTON THIS YEAR! ALBERT Moscrop closed his eyes, drew
back his head and sniffed. It was the long, indulgent sniff of
a man quite absorbed in the olfactory function.

Ah! There it was, unmistakably. A whiff of sea air among
the conflicting odours of the London, Brighton and South
Coast Railway. He pressed a sixpence into a porter's palm.

'D'you see the green portmanteau there on the luggage
rack. Kindly convey it to number fifty, Montpelier Parade,
and inform Miss Lyle that Mr. Moscrop intends to pass the
day on the promenade and will arrive for tea at four. No,
not this one.' He moved his hand protectively to a small
Gladstone bag. 'I shall require this during the day.'

Yes, by George! If Brighton in September lived up to its
reputation he would need the bag. The signs were promising enough. As the train had steamed into the terminus
the crowds on the platform were three and four deep. Third

class passengers every one; there was no doubt of that. Each group carrying its own luggage and every face lobster-red from the sun. Clerks and shop-assistants and their families returning to the fogs of the Metropolis after a week at the 'briny'. They were leaving in hundreds, abandoning the town like an army in retreat, wooden spades and tin buckets in hand. The Brighton of ginger beer and Punch and Judy was being surrendered to a different class of visitor. It was polo at Preston Park and Bernhardt at the Theatre Royal from now on. If you wanted a furnished house in the Royal Crescent the price had jumped overnight to ten guineas a month. The Season had begun.

'Brighton 'Erald?'

'Carry yer bag, mister?'

'Fetch yer cab, sir?'

Small boys bombarded him at the station entrance. New arrivals were worth pursuing in September. He shook his head emphatically. What could be more Philistine than taking one's first breath of ozone from a hansom? He set off at a sharp step down the Queen's Road.

And instantly regretted it. The thoroughfare was lined with public houses of the most dubious kind, the first resort of excursionists when they streamed out of the London trains on Bank Holidays. No gentleman would be seen in such a place. Misspelt postcards, propped at the bottom of windows among dead flies, announced equivocally that rooms with private service were available on request. Winking females reinforced the offer from open casements upstairs.

Odious as the neighbourhood was, Moscrop had made his decision. There was no turning back. He marched down the hill at infantry-pace, eyes concentrated ahead on the convergence of the two sides of the street. Presently, fortitude was rewarded. A wedge of wholesome, glittering blue appeared. By then he was almost as far down as West Street. Salubrious, sea-level Brighton lay ahead.

He did not stop until the sea stretched across the full width of his vision and a fresh breeze ruffled his hair and moustache. He stood at the Esplanade railing listening to the grate of shingle and the cries of children and rediscovering the smell of seaweed. The blood quickened in his veins. He tightened his grip on the Gladstone bag.

The beach below was not crowded by Saturday standards. There were sufficient customers to keep the boatmen and bathing-machine attendants busy, but the real shoulder-to-shoulder occupation of the pebbles was over for 1882. Those remaining were middle-class families for the most part, seated placidly at decent distances from each other, enjoying the air and avoiding the sun under large hats and parasols. A few stone-throwers played ducks and drakes at the water's edge. The summer spectacle of lines of cockney paddlers, boots suspended from their necks, was over. Anyone venturing into the water now came from a Corporation machine, properly attired in a striped costume.

Moscrop joined the general movement in the direction of the West Pier. In his check suit and bowler he was soon inconspicuous, one of a long parade of freshly-arrived visitors taking that first bracing turn along the prom. The tempo was leisurely, dictated by bath-chairs; the conversation loud and entirely taken up with a social roll-call. *Everyone* was expected back from Trouville or Baden-Baden this week or next. The *Fashionable Visitors' List* Office in East Street had never received so many callers.

He looked about him, among the nodding parasols. Really those resonant accents were deceiving. Three-quarters of his fellow-promenaders had not *arrived* socially. They strolled determinedly among the elite, scanning the faces approaching from the Hove direction in hopes of someone recognising them. Moscrop preferred to make a detailed observation of those nearest him. Odd how satisfying it was to spot a slightly faded blazer or a fraying hem. Oh, he was no fashion-plate himself, but he had no pretensions of being one. He had a more original reason for taking a promenade.

In recent years he had made a small pastime of mingling with crowds. Often he left his shop in London's Oxford Street and shambled along the pavement with the throng as far as Marble Arch for the pleasure it gave him. At weekends he liked to visit the Crystal Palace, not to watch fireworks, but to stand among thousands. He thought of Waterloo Station as his club, quite the most congenial place in London. Morning and evening, when the activity there was at its height, he was invariably seated below the clock, reading *The Times*.

His looks were ideally suited to his hobby. His features were undistinguished in every way. You could not possibly spot him in a crowd. But his face was adaptable to each vagary of fashion. When half London went in for luxuriant Dundreary whiskers, Albert Moscrop's growth conformed exactly to the ideal. And when in the seventies the clean-shaven face framed under a central parting became high *ton*, his physiognomy was equal to it. He passed two days at work before anyone noticed the change.

Now, behind the blond moustache and with sidewhiskers scrupulously trimmed level with each ear-lobe, he was all that a man in his forties was required to be. Perhaps he tended to stoop a little when relaxed, but it happened too rarely to be a threat. He was constantly on guard against idiosyncrasies.

There was excitement ahead. Even a few nicely modulated squeals of terror. Knowledgeable promenaders explained to their escorts that the gun-shots they could hear came from a rifle and pistol saloon under the West Pier. Thrills unbounded! Treading the planks of a pier was hair-raising enough, without guns discharging underneath. Moscrop savoured the polite hysteria around him like chalybeate water. He wryly observed that no one actually turned back. Even the faintest hearts were wrapping their gowns across their fronts in readiness for the turnstile.

As he passed inside, he was careful to hold his bag at chest height. Once through, he strode the wooden causeway with a springy step. What better two-pennyworth existed than these three hundred and seventy yards, projecting audaciously across beach and foam and shallows to the deeper waters, indifferent to the power that surged and sucked beneath?

The genius in the design was a revelation. Oh, he had studied his gazetteer conscientiously enough on the way down in the train, read the description of Eusebius Birch's pier, but it had not prepared him for this. It was a triumph of modern architecture, worthy to stand with Scott's St. Pancras Station. Such massive stability, refined by the most intricate detail! He moved left for an unimpeded view. The side stretched away towards the pier-head with the neatness of a perspective exercise. Seating was provided along its full extent, the safety railing serving a second function as a back-support. And here Birch's genius was manifest. The principle of perpendicularity, so fundamental to pier-construction, was abandoned. The railing was bow-shaped. Why? So that a lady could sit against it with comfort and watch the action of the waves beneath her, confident that her posture presented an elegant, undulating line.

It was without question the most civilised pier he had promenaded.

He moved on towards the pier-head, enjoying the drumming of hundreds of sets of shoe-leather on the wooden flooring, more musical to him than the strains of the band ahead. Last August Bank Holiday, according to the newspapers, seventeen thousand visitors had passed through the turnstiles. He had spent the day at London Bridge Station and he was prepared to believe the figure.

Seventeen thousand were not on the pier at one time, of course, exquisite as that might have been. But the ability of the structure to support large numbers was beyond question. From his position there was a comforting view of massive iron piles and girders supporting the projecting sides of the pier-head. They were black as Hades and barnacle-encrusted and the sea bristled with them, thrusting upwards from their concrete foundations. After he had watched them for a minute while the water lapped fitfully at their base, the pier's white superstructure, all domes and bunting, seemed ridiculously slight.

The pier-head, the goal of promenaders, rewarded them with a choice of distractions. As a professional salesman, Moscrop admired the enterprise behind the amusements, even if they were not much to his taste. Beyond the bandstand were four ornamented houses: Snelling's Bazaar; Cheesman's Reading Room and Lending Library; a shell and fossil shop; and Mr. Swaysland's Natural History Museum. The last was particularly popular; besides the stuffed bird exhibition, billed as including a golden eagle and *The Death and Burial of Cock Robin Ornithologically Illustrated*, there was an aviary below the level of the pier-head with thirty live owls which you visited by descending an iron staircase. Moscrop was one of the few who forewent that experience.

Instead he took a rapid turn round the perimeter, learned from notices that the sun's rays would be concentrated on the touch-hole of the pier cannon at noon and that the Diver would descend at 3.30 p.m., and then started back along the east side, from which he had come. The deck was divided by a wood and glass weather-screen, admirable protection against unexpected gusts, but a barrier to movement between the sides. The prospect of Hove and Cliftonville from the pier-head interested him less than Brighton and Kemp Town, so it was logical to return by the same side.

This time he stopped a few yards along, as if to study the serpentine decoration on one of the lamp-standards. Then he placed his bag on the seat and sat beside it in the sunshine, facing inwards towards the weather-screen. Two elderly men reposed in bath-chairs in its shadow. He observed them steadily for several minutes, undistracted by the promenaders crossing his line of vision. Satisfied that they were deep in slumber, he turned towards the sea.

It was so dazzling after the shaded scene opposite that his eyes contracted at once. Turning his face from the myriad glittering specks below the horizon, he scanned the browner water inshore and the waves languidly breaking below the pier, producing a marbling effect as the foam dispersed. There were other sights to interest a pier-goer: excursion-yachts, fishing-boats, the pleasure steamer twenty minutes out from the head and passing the old Chain Pier. Moscrop took them in with one sweep of the head and moved his gaze to the shore.

It was not architecture that caught his attention now, not the endless facade of white-fronted hotels and Georgian houses, nor the stately sweep of the King's Road and the Marine Parade. It was the beach. More precisely it was the people on the beach.

His position afforded an outstanding view of the shingle and its occupants as far as the Chain Pier, almost a mile distant. There were none of the obstructions one encountered from other viewpoints. The stone groynes hid nothing from this height and the bathing-machines were like rows of match-boxes. The sunshine and the approach of noon had brought numbers of visitors on to the beach. The pebbles, as brown as the Gobi when you saw them *en masse*, were studded with the brilliant colours of shawls and parasols. There must have been four or five hundred people within view. He flushed with exhilaration.

He turned away, his tongue moistening his upper lip. His two neighbours slept on and the parade along the deck continued, unheeding. He reached for the Gladstone bag.

It was going to be so much easier than it had ever been before. The conditions were perfect: range, light, elevation. He hesitated only to select the best instrument for his purpose. The sporting model by Burrows of Malvern was the least conspicuous and the new Carl Zeiss was the most powerful, but he settled for his Prussian Officer's field-instrument with a magnification of eight diameters. He could not be sure that his hand was steady enough this morning for the strongest lenses. Where was the profit in ten diameters if every tremor were magnified ten times?

He withdrew a small square of velvet from his pocket. There was no need to hurry. Now that he was seated, nobody looked his way. He was accepted as a lounger, and like the bandsmen and the anglers on the pier-head he had merged with the scenery. He breathed on each eye-piece and polished it methodically with the velvet.

When the cleaning was finished, he folded the velvet and replaced it in his pocket. Then he turned, rested his elbows on the rail, trained the glasses on the pleasure-steamer in the middle distance and stroked the image expertly into perfect focus. He watched a gull fly across the wording *S.S. Brighton* on the bow. By Jove! Those Prussians knew how to grind a lens. Small wonder the French had lost the war.

But he had not brought out the binoculars to study shipping. He moved his field of view across the flexuous lines of the Chain Pier and on to the beach below the Marine Parade. Without adjusting the focus, he continued the movement slowly left, scanning the steep banks of shingle. His eyes received only a blurred impression of shapes and colours, with a figure once or twice stealing into the picture when its movement momentarily matched the sweep of the glass.

That was incidental. He was not concerned with individuals yet. He swung the glass over everything contained in the entire length of beach within his purview: upturned fishing-boats, blackened breakwaters, nets spread to dry, garish bathing-machines, seaweed in heaps, fluttering pennants and hundreds of reclining people, all merging in an optical effect as dazzling and devoid of form as Turner's last landscapes.

The binoculars reached the limit of their sweep, the pier itself, close to hand and out of focus. The image went blank and Moscrop shifted the instrument away from his eyes and rested his chin upon it contentedly. He had achieved nothing in the way of observation—the movement along the shore-line was far too quick for that—but his purpose was otherwise. It was the gesture that had mattered, a little piece of ritual, quite personal in significance. He had measured the area within his sights and staked a claim, so to speak. A mile or so of Brighton beach was subject to the scrutiny of his lens. The glasses had passed, however briefly, over every man, woman and child who chanced to be there this morning. Encouraged by this, he took out his piece of velvet and set to work again, humming an accompaniment to the brass band behind him.

For no very clear reason, he thought about the young woman who had sat opposite him in the carriage on the way down, a pretty, fair-haired creature in a white muslin dress and straw hat trimmed with crimson. Yet it was more about himself that he thought. How he had covertly stolen glimpses of the girl, not wishing to give offence, peering into the window to catch her reflection in the glass each time the train passed through a cutting. He was not shy—the proprietor of a shop could not afford to be—but the enforced intimacy of a First Class carriage was different altogether from the business-like exchanges in his Oxford Street emporium. When the train had approached Clayton tunnel, he had got up to fasten the window and she had nodded her appreciation of the courtesy. In the darkness he had set his eyes firmly in her direction, hopeful that a chink of light might illuminate her features for an instant. He had even strained forward to catch the fragrance she wore. But when the light returned he was stiffly back against the headrest with his eyes trained on the procession of telegraph poles past the window. How odd it was that if the same young woman were now seated on the beach he could observe her minutely without embarrassment on either side!

For his first concentrated survey he chose the area of beach below the Grand Hotel. The building's height made it the obvious point of reference. If you did not use some kind of landmark you would lose yourself on the beach just as surely as if you were tramping aimlessly through the shingle. He brought the glasses into sharp focus on one of the Italianate balconies and moved the field of view slowly down the edge of the building that adjoined Hobden's Royal Tepid Swimming Baths for Gentlemen. A landau passed across the image; he had reached the level of the King's Road. He dipped the binoculars lower, down the Esplanade wall to the top tier of white-painted bathing-machines. He continued the movement without pausing. Whatever else he may have been, he was no Peeping Tom. The sight of a shapely ankle or a foam-drenched petticoat-hem exposed to the sun to dry was a side-benefit of his researches, but he drew the line at peering into bathing-machines. That was a misapplication of science.

Pebbles monopolised the scene now, more blue than brown when he saw them closely, and as clean as if every one had been scrubbed that day. Farther down was an upturned fishing-boat on trestles, with children scrambling over it. They were the first live figures the lens had caught and he was pleased at the definition. Some loss of colour was inevitable, but the features were sharp and there was no spectral fringe around them. The Zeiss itself could not have produced a clearer image.

He discovered a courting couple sitting against a rowing-boat, the girl in a white serge and navy-blue yachting dress with silver anchor buttons (could he really see that well or was his imagination supplying the details?) and a pill-box hat, and the man in ducks, sharing her parasol. The chaperone, heavily veiled and knitting assiduously, sat with her back against the stern. To their right was a poorer family who seemed to have missed the exodus. They were eating shrimps or whelks and passing round a stone bottle, presumably of beer. A fruit-seller approached and just as quickly moved on.

The band to Moscrop's rear stopped playing. All that was audible now was the thud of footfalls on the planking and the lapping of the tide. It made an odd accompaniment to the animated scene he was observing. With one faculty increasingly involved in the life below him, the others had become dissociated from what was happening on the pier. The music had blended pleasingly with the images, but now that it had stopped he was straining to hear the crunch of pebbles as someone walked by and the shrill cries of the children playing on the boat. It was like being afflicted suddenly with deafness. His concentration was going.

Then with that happy facility optical instruments have for chancing on the unexpected, the glasses isolated a young woman of riveting attractiveness. She was three-quarters turned away from the lens and wearing a hat of fine, white straw with an outrageously wide brim which dipped and obscured her face at each step she took. She was making her way up the steep shelf of pebbles towards the bathing-machines. Difficult as this should have been, her movements were a delight to the eye, arms gently see-sawing and hips buoyantly triumphing over the unstable footing. Moscrop could not claim many sights of the fair sex negotiating banks of shingle, but the ascent into a hansom was a not dissimilar exercise which he had observed quite regularly. Never in all his life had he seen the female form move so becomingly as this. She was fractionally out of focus—or was it his breath on the object-glass?—but he was quite incapable of making any adjustment.

She wore one of the white muslin shawls currently in fashion, over a lilac-coloured gown. And she was carrying something white, with pink stripes. A bath towel. Was she going to bathe? He hoped not. It would be too much, all at once. No, she was walking towards the men's machines, by Heaven, and going up to the blue-uniformed attendant!

The fellow spoke with her for a moment and she put something in his hand. He touched his cap and accepted the towel from her. Now she was walking away, down the beach, and Moscrop had to keep her in view and miss seeing what the attendant did with the towel.

The hat still flounced distractingly, but from this direction more of her face was visible, framed by black hair cut square over her brow and loosely knotted behind. She was not conventionally good-looking. Too wide in the mouth and high in the cheek-bone. And she was no child. Thirty, he guessed. Perhaps he was already bewitched, because it seemed to him at that moment that a wide mouth and high cheek-bones were exactly what every young woman should have and that thirty was the perfect age to be.

And then the spell broke. There was a most appalling crash, as if the pier itself had collapsed. The shock jolted the glasses from Moscrop's hands. They were saved only by the retaining-strap about his neck. He turned in a frenzy of indignation. One of the two sleepers across the deck was calling to him.

'The cannon, y'know. The pier cannon. The sun's rays fire it at the meridian. It's twelve, you can depend upon it. I propose to synchronise my watch.'

Moscrop had already turned and clamped the binoculars to his eyes, all caution abandoned now. The tragedy was that when he had followed the young woman down the beach he had neglected his bearings altogether. As he cast about with the glasses in an agony of frustration, he knew already that he had lost her and might as well never have fixed his lens upon her.

CHAPTER 2

PRESENTLY HE STOWED THE glasses in his bag and rejoined the promenade along the deck. He needed to compose himself. Public promenading was the best remedy he knew for a mind in turmoil. He took a position behind a taller, more conspicuous man in a top hat and gave all his attention to achieving a similar stride-length while maintaining the proper, erect posture. He was at once incorporated in the general movement towards the pier-head.

Confound it, a man of his age and experience didn't fall for the first handsome female to cross the face of his lens. Unthinkable. Could ruin his holiday from the start. No harm in using her to check his alignment, but that should be the end of it, and no regrets when the image changed. If he was honest with himself, she was not even worth using as a range-finder. Damn it, you couldn't do anything with a moving focal object. He had acted in a most unprofessional manner. He rubbed his moustache with the full vigour of a penitent.

It was not even arguable that she was beautiful. Hers were not the cast of features one saw engraved in the *Tatler*. She wouldn't turn many heads, with a complexion as dark as that and lips so prominent that already he was forgetting the rest of her face. Besides, she was definitely several inches too short for a woman. It wouldn't do at all for a man of his stature to take an interest in under-sized women. That was where binoculars let you down, unless you made a point of checking proportions. You *couldn't* be too careful. He preened the moustache with his fingertips, more reconciled now. It had been a salutary experience.

The smell of powder lingered round the cannon as he passed it, his thoughts firmly on optical techniques.

She was almost certainly married. Single women of thirty didn't gad about public beaches unaccompanied.

Next time he would use the Zeiss. For all its clarity, the Prussian instrument had a smaller objective lens. There were undoubted advantages in a wider field of view.

For a small woman, she had made quick progress up the pebbles. The banking was steep for a short pair of under-standings to negotiate, yet she had managed it quite easily, and with such grace! Could he conceivably have underestimated her height?

An interesting technical problem. If the alignment were even fractionally wrong in the Prussian Officer's field glasses, there was likely to have been distortion. At that range, and allowing for the moment of the image. . . . What wouldn't he give for a sighting with the Zeiss! Yet even if he devoted the rest of the afternoon to scanning the beach there was small chance of pinpointing her again. One didn't even have the pink-striped towel to focus on.

Moscrop stopped. The towel! Why the devil hadn't he thought of it? He *did* have the towel to focus on. It was down there somewhere among the bathing-machines. She had given it to the attendant. Find the towel and he had a positive link with the woman!

In seconds he was back at the side of the pier, skimming the glasses over the facade of the Grand to locate the right machines. One attendant usually had a dozen to patrol, no more. If he could identify the man. . . . Ah! Splendid! There was the fellow, bless his blue uniform, standing by his chalked list of prices. If sixpence bought half an hour's hire there was a good chance that the bather in need of the pink-striped towel was not far away. In fact, to Moscrop's profound satisfaction, a flash of pink and white appeared in his field of view as he moved the glasses on to the fourth machine. The towel was hanging over the open door like an ensign. The bather, apparently, had still to return from his swim.

Moscrop surveyed the strip of beach between the machines and the water's edge. The lens defined a number of seated groups, but the only standing figures were small children and a group of itinerant musicians. The expected form in bathing-drawers stumbling over the stones was nowhere in evidence. However, several heads were bobbing in the water. No doubt the owner of the towel was so enjoying his dip that he was prepared to pay another sixpence.

He put down his glasses and made a calculation. At a rough and ready estimate the distance from where he was standing to the point on the esplanade nearest to the bathing-machine was not more than a quarter of a mile. If he stepped out briskly he could be there, in a matchless viewing position, before the bather got back to his machine. Even if his judgement were wrong, the fellow could hardly have towelled himself, changed and left before he reached there.

He set off along the pier at a purposeful step, zigzagging for faster progress, his bag swinging outwards towards hapless promenaders as he went by. At the toll-gate he was approached by a photographer and almost bowled the man over. Photographs! *A Permanent Memento of Your Visit to Brighton.* Heavens! He had no intention of being exposed to a photographer's lens at any time, least of all now. At the King's Road he steered through the crowd gathered round a French string band and almost ran along the Esplanade to the front of the Grand.

He had, of course, glanced frequently to his right as he came, to check whether a bather emerged from the water. He had seen none, but there were points on the route where his view was obstructed. In a situation such as this, he told himself, an element of risk was inevitable. It was a relief to reach the section of Esplanade overlooking the machine in question, and it was in the nature of a personal triumph when he observed through a gap that the towel still hung unclaimed on the open door.

Nonchalantly propping his right foot on the lowest cross-piece of the Esplanade railing, he took out his Zeiss and focused it on the sea. There was no need now to feel self-conscious about using binoculars. He simply joined the ranks of telescopists at intervals along the sea-wall from Cliftonville to Kemp Town, observing everything that disturbed the surface of the water. Peering out to sea was becoming as fashionable as bicycling along the front. Now he understood why his sales of optical instruments that summer had been the highest for years.

A murmur of pleasure escaped him at the quality of image the Zeiss produced. Every detail of a distant excursion-yacht was defined with diamond sharpness. Unhappily, though, the water nearer the shore where the waves were breaking was hidden from view by the steep bank of shingle. The bathers were invisible unless they ventured beyond the shallows. He put down the glasses and trusted natural vision to give him the first sighting of whoever came to claim the towel. On the beach, scores of small groups basked in the noon sun, read novels or studied the horizon, oblivious of the vigil being kept from behind.

Minutes later, a head and shoulders appeared above the ridge of shingle, moving upwards and forwards. By degrees, the figure emerged in full, slimly built, narrow-shouldered and wrapped in a beach-robe extending to the ankles. Had he not noticed that the female bathing-machines were situated many yards to the right, Moscrop would have doubted whether he was watching a man at all. He put the Zeiss to his eyes again.

The brilliance of the noon sun refracted by the waves made observation uncertain until the background was entirely of pebbles. Then there was no difficulty in identifying the bather as a youth of fourteen or fifteen. He put down the glasses. He was not looking for a boy. No connection was conceivable between a lad of that age and a married

woman of thirty. His eyes travelled back across the stones to
the line that divided land and water.

Yet there was something that fretted his concentration.
What the devil was it? He glanced down again. The boy
was approaching the machines, sidling between parasols
clustered about the beach like monstrous fungi spawned by
the morning sun. Such colours! The most garish combina-
tions seemed acceptable in this light and setting. People
never seen in anything but dark suits and white shirts could
sport utterly outlandish stripes on a beach and appear perfectly at ease. Why, just to look at the robe the boy was
wearing. . . .

Moscrop looked. The robe had pink and white stripes. It
was made of the same stuff as the towel.

He gripped the binoculars, half-lifted them to his eyes and
put them down again. He was too near for that. He watched
in dazed incomprehension as the boy walked to the bathing-
machine, flicked the towel clear of the door and began rubbing his hair. Deuced extraordinary: the youth was too old
to be the woman's son and certainly too young. . . . Moscrop
closed his eyes and shook his head in a quivering movement,
expelling an unacceptable thought from his mind.

He occupied himself winding the strap around the
glasses, clapping them into their case and fastening the
buckles, performing each movement crisply, as if reacting
to orders. Sometimes simple actions were a spur to decision. If he could summon the strength of purpose, this was
the moment to pick up his bag and walk away along the
promenade. No woman was worth the indignity of waiting
for a fifteen-year-old boy to put on his clothes and following

him along a public beach. He had never done such a thing in his life.

The picture of her picking her way up the pebbles flashed into his mind's eye again. Perhaps, after all, he would spend a few more minutes standing here. There was an incomparable view of the pier. Was it possible, he wondered, to identify each of the flags between the toll-towers and the pier-head? Now it chanced that the standard of India was directly above the bathing-machine in his line of view, and that when his eyes reached it, his attention was deflected by the youth standing quite still on the steps, enjoying the sensation of the sun on his limbs before retreating inside. He seemed to be indulging in some youthful fantasy, striking the pose of an athlete or pugilist, the towel loosely draped about his neck, the robe drawn back from his chest. His face was in profile, chin jutting forward. It occurred to Moscrop that this was a face he could not bring himself to like. It was not the self-satisfaction in the boy's expression; that went with the pose and was forgivable. No, it was the cut of the features that repelled him. They were neat enough, to be sure. Handsome even. A broad, high forehead, well-formed eyebrows, fine, tapered nose, manly chin. The hair straight and strikingly blond. The mouth, too, balanced the other features, but Moscrop descried a hint of coarseness in the lower lip, the merest superfluity of flesh betraying (to a trained observer) intimations of sensuousness. Where had he seen a mouth of that cast before?—in some disagreeable context, he was certain. While he considered the point, the youth turned his head slightly, following the flight of a seabird. The movement afforded Moscrop a view of the boy's eyes. They were large and heavy-lidded and protruding, giving the face an unseemly, almost wanton aspect. He placed them at once: they were the eyes of the young man in *The Awakening Conscience*, a painting of Holman Hunt's, depicting a girl resisting a lover's invitation to seat herself on his lap. If one mentally stripped away the young man's whiskers, the likeness to the boy in the bathing-robe was disturbingly apparent. Child as he was, his eyes and mouth, those twin betrayers of the darkest instincts, conveyed the same callousness the artist had expressed in his portrait of the seducer.

The boy turned and let himself into the bathing-machine. Moscrop produced a silk handkerchief and wiped his brow. Good Lord! What a lather he was getting himself into! It was utterly ridiculous. What did it matter whom the boy looked like? He was no more than a link in the present chain of circumstances. He could resemble anyone from Charles Peace to Mr. Gladstone himself and it would not matter a jot. Once he had made contact with the fair provider of the towel he ceased to be of any importance.

But when some ten minutes later the youth descended from the machine, carrying his roll of bathing garments, paid the attendant and crunched away across the stones, it was not to rendezvous with anyone on the beach. Instead he mounted the nearest steps to the Esplanade and headed away in the direction of the West Pier. There was nothing for it but to set off in pursuit. Laden as he was with his bag of optical instruments and scarcely recovered from his exertions in covering the same route from the reverse direction, Moscrop found the pace damnably fast. The boy was short of stature—though probably not for his age—and would soon have been indistinguishable in the press of promenaders ahead, were it not for the red blazer he wore, matched by a brilliant silk boater-ribbon.

By the pier entrance, where the crowd was thickest, he lost him. At another time it would have given him boundless pleasure to edge his way into the throng, regardless of whether he were joining a group buying brandy-balls or those trying to listen to the band. Today he skirted the crowd, anxiously seeking his quarry. Then—what relief!—he spotted the strip of red across the road. But—consternation!—the boy was paying for the hire of a bicycle. Moscrop had not used the two-wheel mode of transport in the whole of his life.

He did the only thing possible: crossed the King's Road and ran to the cab-stand. Already the boy was aloft and in process of achieving sufficient momentum, with the assistant's support, to sustain his own balance. The bathing things were in a convenient basket attached to the saddle. He passed the cab-stand at a wobble, but in independent motion. Moscrop took off his bowler and beat it against his thigh in exasperation. There was not a cab within hail.

It was five minutes at least before a growler drew up and disgorged its passenger. Five minutes! A bicyclist could be halfway to Kemp Town in that time. He mounted the carriage steps before he was aware that a second passenger, a Pekinese dog, had still to descend. He almost threw it into its owner's arms and ordered the cabman to drive away.

Progress along the King's Road was desperately slow. Nobody wanted to hurry; the drive along the front was an opportunity to be seen, not to raise dust. So the cab went at little faster than the pace of the goat-chaises carrying parties of small children between the piers. There was nothing to be gained from urging the cabman to go faster; the volume of traffic made that impossible unless you had your own horse or bicycle.

The quite charming views to left and right, the elegant Regency facades and the splendidly green sea, were lost on Moscrop. He was craning to look past the cabman at any snatch of red in prospect and being deceived by parasols and toy balloons all the way to the Chain Pier. There he ordered the cab to halt. He had seen a rack with some half-dozen bicycles against the wall of a building adjoining the pier entrance. One machine was being pushed into position there by a boy no taller than the front wheel. There was a basket attached to the saddle. Moscrop gave the cabman his shilling and cut across the road.

'This bicycle,' he demanded of the boy. 'Who returned it to you?'

'It's from up the West Pier, guv. This 'ere's as far as you can go for a tanner. Gent 'ired it up there and brought it in 'ere. I just collect 'em and stable 'em. Quite a few geezers ride up 'ere regular for lunch at Mutton's or the Aquarium. Some of 'em try riding back after. Rare sight that is, if they've had a jug or two of four-ale.'

'The person who hired it,' persisted Moscrop. 'Would you recall whether he was a young man not much older than yourself and wearing a red blazer?'

The boy scratched his chin. 'Can't say as I can recall anything.'

Moscrop put his hand in his pocket.

'Now that I put me mind to it,' said the boy resourcefully, ''e *was* wearing a blazer. And it were red all right.'

Moscrop thrust a sixpence between their faces. It flashed in the sunlight. 'Which way did this young man go?'

'Up there, guv. The Aquarium, I reckon. Ah, much obliged to you.'

The Aquarium! He was more accustomed to studying life *beside* the sea than in it, but he did not hesitate. He was across the road, past the terrace garden and up to the turn-stile under the Aquarium clocktower before the bicycle boy had put the sixpence in his pocket.

CHAPTER 3

ADMISSION TO THE AQUARIUM was a shilling. Half a crown spent in two minutes! Indulging one's curiosity was an expensive pastime. He hoped the information he had bought at the bicycle-stand was reliable. Even if it were, the finding of the youth would not be easy. The forecourt at the foot of the granite steps he was descending was like an hotel foyer, thick with visitors noisily debating whether they would first take lunch, see the exhibits or listen to the conservatory orchestra. He paused midway down, scrutinising the shaded areas under the red-brick arches and behind the terracotta columns. The only red coats in view belonged to members of the militia. He moved on and down and crossed the pavement to the entrance-hall.

This too was crowded, but less noisy. It was furnished as a reading-room, with long tables. Visitors had come there in dozens and gone to the London newspapers like men

overboard to lifebelts. However well a landlady prepared
breakfast, it was not the same without *The Morning Post*.

The current editions of Brighton's seventeen daily and
weekly papers, liberally arranged along the eighty-foot length
of the hall, were not much in demand. The single exception
was *The Fashionable Visitors' List*. For every one studying that
journal, three or four waited to replace him. Suitably, it was
mounted under glass on an elongated lectern. At another
table, the latest telegrams were dissected by a small colony of
holiday-makers from the London Stock Exchange.

Moscrop stood in uncertainty, trying to make the same
decision that provoked such discussion outside. Should he turn
left and enter the restaurant or go forward into the main
aquarium? He was already satisfied that the boy was not
in the reading-room. It was fair to presume that if he was
in the building at all he had come there to meet someone.
Perhaps he had already met them outside and gone into the
restaurant. If he had, he should be there for a considerable
while; long enough to make it safe to search the corridors
housing the tanks. He stepped forward decisively.

He was unprepared for the next experience. After the
babble outside, the clublike concentration in the reading-
room had presented a contrast, but it was at least recognis-
able as another aspect of modern life. The aquarium was
not. It was other-worldly. Dimly-lit aisles extended before
him like cloisters in a Fra Angelico fresco. Pillars of deeply
coloured serpentine marble, Bath stone and red Edinburgh
granite supported a groined roof stretching ahead for more
than two hundred feet. It was formed of variegated bricks,
crossed by finely moulded Gothic vaulting. The impression

on Moscrop was profound; he would not have blinked an eye if an organ had started to play and a clerical procession walked past. He was ready to accept that a patch of light on the pavement to his left was filtered through a stained-glass window. It seemed sacreligious to discover that it came from a gas-lit tank of lobsters.

He paced the corridor uneasily, peering ahead for a glimpse of the boy, but feeling obliged to simulate some interest in the tanks, rather as one casts an eye over tomb-stones on a cathedral tour. A skate came close to the glass of one and hovered there, a grotesque parody of a human face, with wicked twinkling eyes and mocking mouth. Mackerel and herrings played among the rising bubbles. Bass dived repeatedly into the fine grit at the bottom of their tank, rolling themselves in it with evident relish. In the main tank, over a hundred feet long, porpoises darted easily from end to end. A line of visitors watched in hushed amazement at such quicksilver velocity contained within a foot of their faces.

Halfway along the corridor there was still no glimpse of red in the line of shuffling visitors. He kept towards the centre, near the small tanks of tropical fish mounted on pedestals. He smiled wryly at one labelled *Shanghai Telescope Fish*. Newtonian or Cassegrainian? Whichever they were, they would find it a challenge to produce any image at all in this dim underworld. No telescope he knew could retain sufficient light to be of any use here.

To his right he noticed a passage leading to a separate exhibit. *The New Alligator and Crocodile Cavern is now completed and Open to the Public* announced a board beside it. He hesitated. Might such a curiosity interest a boy of fifteen? He supposed it would. As a meeting-place, however, it was a singularly unlikely choice. She of the fluttering white hat was impossible to imagine making a rendezvous in a reptile-house.

He reviewed the line of visitors filing past the tanks. Several straw boaters were prominent. Not a single red blazer. There was nothing for it but to try the Crocodile Cavern.

The interior was darker than the main aquarium. Hissing gas-jets situated at floor-level threw a yellowish light over indeterminate areas of mud and vegetation. He waited at the entrance, accustoming his eyes to the conditions. Reassured that there was actually a four-foot barrier of iron and glass between the human and reptilian occupants of the cavern, he stepped forward. It was as crowded as the bar in a music hall. Instead of shouting for drinks, the customers passed the time peering downwards, telling crocodiles from logs of wood. Saturday afternoon zoologists. He had no desire to join in, but to see anything at all he needed to gain a place at the glass. And getting there was certainly harder than ordering drinks at the Alhambra. Those at the front refused to move on before observing some sign of life in the tank, and the reptiles were not disposed to co-operate.

At length he wedged himself between a clergyman and a large woman in a plush hat. To establish his interest in crocodiles, he tossed a penny over the glass on to the back of an unblinking twelve-footer. Then he looked along the barrier at the line of human faces to his right. The light directed upwards from the tank caught the undersides of their features. Chins, lips, noses and eyebrows were illuminated in the manner of murderers' effigies in Madame Tussaud's. He sighed. In these conditions you would be hard put to it to recognise your own mother.

There was a small stir at the far end of the barrier. A child was being held up for a better view, a boy of two or three in a white cotton sailor-suit. Tiny, fat fingers gripped the edge of the glass above the heads of the onlookers. A shock of flaxen curls appeared behind them and was helped above the glass, to project over the top, giving the child a bird's-eye view of the crocodiles. He was supported at the ankles. From where Moscrop was, it looked an uncomfortable vantage point. And so it appeared to someone else, for a young woman was protesting actively, trying to haul the child down to a safer height. 'No, Master Guy, he don't like it. He don't like it at all. Can't you see he don't like it? Put him down, for pity's sake.' From her dress and manner, she was the child's nursemaid, quite properly demonstrating her concern for its safety. Master Guy was unimpressed, though. He edged the ankles higher, beyond her reach. The weight of the child's head began to draw it downwards. One of the reptiles in the tank moved. The girl screamed. Several sets of hands at once combined to pull the child to safety. It seemed quite unharmed. Probably it had never been at risk. There is nothing like a scream in a reptile-house to lead people to hasty conclusions. Certainly the young man named Guy was treating the matter lightly, laughingly ruffling the curls that were now drawn implacably to the nursemaid's bosom.

Moscrop watched him with increasing interest, not because the incident was of any importance, but because now that the child was reunited with its nurse, he could see for the first time what Master Guy was wearing: a blazer, flattened against the glass by a sudden concentration of pressure from the crowd and caught in the gaslight as red as a signal-flag. What luck! He backed away from the barrier at once to the back of the crowd and moved as near as he could.

'Be reasonable, Bridget, dammit,' he heard from in front. 'Anyone would think from your behaviour I was trying to get rid of the child, like someone in the police reports.' The voice was pitched high and carried well. Whatever Bridget thought, the crowd would be left in no doubt about the young man's good intentions. 'The boy wanted to see the brutes for himself. Part of his education. You'll have to keep a check on yourself, my girl, or you'll get us into no end of trouble, won't she, young Jason?' If it was the youth Moscrop had followed from the bathing-station, he spoke with a self-assurance beyond his years.

A shifting of positions among the crowd settled the issue. The wearer of the blazer emerged within a yard of Moscrop, girl and child in tow. His hand lingered automatically among young Jason's curls, but his eyes, what was visible of them in the shadows, glinted in a most unrepentant way. *The Awakening Conscience!* Beyond any doubt it was the boy from the beach. Moscrop stepped in behind, resolved not to lose him again.

In the main aquarium, the light that had seemed poor before was as good as daylight now. They crossed a central vestibule and entered the second part of the main aisle, Moscrop keeping within twenty yards of them. Their step was business-like. Tank after tank was passed without the inmates receiving even the compliment of a glance.

He presently became aware of a sound from the end of the building, a persistent throbbing, soon detectable as the percussionist's contribution to a waltz-tune. It sounded curiously unsuited to the surroundings, even when the full orchestra was audible. To their credit, the aquarium managers had provided a small forest of palm trees in tubs, to make a distinction between the musicians and the specimens of marine life. Members of the public were making their way there with the resolute tread of Sunday morning church-goers. They were passing straight through into a further room, towards which Guy strode, with the girl a step or two behind, the child now dormant in her arms.

He followed them into a spacious conservatory, well-provided with bentwood and bamboo chairs distributed at random among tall sub-tropical shrubs. Most were turned in the direction of the Aquarium Orchestra, a dozen instrumentalists mounted on a small platform behind a fernery, but a number of the audience elected to promenade around the extremities. There was much to charm the eye: cascades and fountains and miniature Alpine scenery.

Which way had they gone? Heavens, these were practically jungle conditions, with fronds and ferns making it quite impossible to see more than a dozen yards in any direction. 'There is ample seating on the far side, sir,' a bored voice advised him.

'I was—er—with the people ahead. Young fellow in a red blazer.'

A limp hand waved him forward. 'Dr. Prothero's party? To the left of the podium, sir, behind the Chinese magnolia.'

A *doctor.* Who on earth next? At this rate he would soon be pursuing half the population of Brighton. He took in a long, deep breath. It was time to pause, to consider the implications of what he was doing. Spying out the land through the end of a telescope was one thing; running a strange woman to earth quite another. Not at all a healthy way to start a holiday.

Manfully he made an effort to call to mind worthier ways of spending time at Brighton: lunch at Mutton's, bathing at Brill's, concerts at the Dome. None displaced the memory of a large white hat dancing elegantly to the motion of unseen limbs over the shingle. He shrugged, released the breath upwards through the bristles of his moustache and submitted himself to the palms and the Aquarium Orchestra.

And there it was when he rounded the magnolia—the hat in all its magnificence, quite still now, without the suggestion of a tremor during the orchestra's performance.

She was seated in a cane chair, as if for a studio photograph, her face in profile, sharply defined against the dark green of the ferns. Guy and the nursemaid and child had positioned themselves behind and someone else was seated alongside. Moscrop concentrated on her alone. Good Lord, what imperfect instruments binoculars were! The image his lens had produced from the pier conveyed nothing of the texture of that complexion.

He decided to promenade. If he picked a careful route, he would be able to observe her from different angles. He was not the class of man who contrived a clumsy introduction at the first opportunity. Nonchalantly, he set off along a small path that took him behind her. He made a show of examining plants as he walked, but he need not have bothered; she was totally absorbed in the music.

There was a small pond ahead, with a fountain in the centre. It was a perfectly natural action to pause there to look at the goldfish lurking under the lily-pads. Through a gap in the foliage to the left of the jet, he watched the boy Guy stoop to speak something under the hat-brim. She would not like her concentration broken, Moscrop was sure. Confounded bad form to talk during a concert: it confirmed his earlier impression of the boy. How gratifying to see that she silenced the young pup with a single small movement of the right hand. The hat, if he were not mistaken, quivered with the force of her reproof.

He moved on to the next break in the foliage, a promising position, almost directly opposite the point from which he had first seen her. Unfortunately the view was entirely obstructed by her companion, who was now forced on Moscrop's attention for the first time. He was a man of slight build, in his fifties, almost bald. He sat elegantly in a chair which was the twin of hers, his elbows on the arms and the point of his chin resting on a bridge formed by the tips of his index fingers. A well-proportioned physique; posture relaxed, yet entirely under control, down to the crossed ankles and dipped toes. There was no doubting his identity. This was Dr. Prothero: the badge of his profession, his silk hat, lay on his lap ready for all emergencies.

Moscrop sniffed, took a turn round an oleander, strolled back to the pond and looked again at the two seated figures. He was reluctant to consider what relationship they had to each other. He noted merely that there was twenty years' difference in their ages—oh, even twenty-five. Yes, the doctor was assuredly nearly twice her age.

The boy Guy, frustrated in his attempt to speak during the recital, withdrew a pouch from his pocket. Tobacco, at his age? No, by George, it was snuff he was taking, putting

it to his nostril as openly as if he were inhaling camphor!
Boys were boys and it was unrealistic to imagine that they
did not secretly indulge from time to time in smoking-room
practices, but this was in a *public place*, in the company of a
lady. The doctor, for his part, seemed quite indifferent to
what was going on behind him. In fact, it was now apparent
from this angle of observation that he was taking more than
a passing interest in one member of the orchestra, a lady
harpist in a black gown of *décolleté* design. She may well have
been a conspicuously talented musician, of course, but that
did not account for Dr. Prothero's present preoccupation,
because the piece the orchestra were playing had no part at
all for a harp.

The waltz finished with a flourish. The performers acknowl-
edged a ripple of applause with nods and smiles and began
rearranging their music-sheets. It was the opportunity for any
of the seated contingent of the audience who were becoming
restless to move discreetly away. Dr. Prothero already had his
hat on and was making towards the door, unconcerned, apparently, whether the rest of his party were following. When
he did look briefly back, it was merely in the direction of the
orchestra. His companion, for her part, turned to make some
remark to Guy and then rose, rearranged the folds of her skirt
and followed, the others going with her.

Moscrop made his way out by a less direct path. Even
so, he reached the door almost as Guy did, penetrating the
conservatory foliage like Stanley within sight of Ujiji. In
the main aisle outside, it was more difficult to conceal his
pursuit, for there was no cover except the central row of
pillars, and anyone darting between them would seem quite

as curious and exceptional as the fish themselves. He had no choice but to step out at the same brisk rate as Dr. Prothero and his party, and take the chance that if any of them looked round they would think nothing odd about a visitor who followed so hard on their heels.

Not that he need feel guilty in any sense; there was nothing unlawful in what he was doing. He had taken an observer's interest in his fellow-beings for years; wasn't that his hobby, after all? Where was the harm in making oneself anonymous, a face in a crowd or a dot on the landscape, but having the power to pinpoint others, focus a lens on them and study them at will without their ever realising it? The only difference now was that he was putting his anonymity at risk. He was not content to join the crowds shuffling in front of the tanks to right and left. And if he needed any reassurance that the risk was worth taking, it was there in front of him; she was as exquisite at walking pace as she was clambering up the beach. The hat-brim and the folds of her parasol rippled in concert with her quick steps.

The doctor did not pause until he was through the reading-room and at the door of the restaurant. There, a short discussion ensued. Obviously the nursemaid and child could not be taken in for lunch; Bridget was receiving her instructions. Sure enough, Guy was sent to retrieve a small perambulator from behind a potted fern, a chair-like contrivance with three wooden wheels, and the child was fastened into it.

What should he do next—follow them into lunch, hopeful of securing an adjoining table, or wait outside with the nursemaid and child? Were they likely to wait there, for that matter? No, the child would need to be fed. Bridget was already wheeling the pram across the reading-room.

On an impulse he did the thing which seemed the least logical: abandoned the subject of his fascination and followed the servant. It was decided so spontaneously that his movement to the door was executed with complete naturalness. He caught up with Bridget at the foot of the granite steps.

'Allow me, young lady.'

She had no choice. He already had the pram in his hands.

'Oh thank you.' She gave him a coy smile. 'Let me take your bag then, at least.'

'It's heavy.'

'Not so heavy as Jason and his pram. I'm obliged to you, sir.'

'Not at all. He's a bonny child. That was his mother at the restaurant entrance, was it?' Said with the casual air of someone making polite conversation. The girl would know nothing of the significance he attached to the answer.

'Mrs. Prothero? Yes. She's Jason's Mamma.'

'And the older boy? He's not Jason's brother, surely?'

'Ah, but he is. His half-brother, anyway. That's Master Guy. He's fifteen now, and a trying age that is, if he's typical of it.'

'He would be Dr. Prothero's son by a previous wife?'

'Yes. Don't ask me which one. The present Mrs. Prothero's the third. The doctor don't keep his wives long, does he? There we are, then. You're a gentleman, sir, and I'm deeply obliged.'

'No trouble,' said Moscrop. 'No trouble at all.' But as he took back his bag and walked across to the promenade railing, his expression was more than troubled. He wore the look of a man whose worst intimations had been confirmed.

CHAPTER 4

SATURDAY HAD BEEN so fully occupied that Moscrop found himself on Sunday morning at half past ten in the odd predicament of starting out for Morning Service without knowing which of the Brighton churches was a suitable place of worship. St. Stephen's, in Montpelier Place, looked convenient; indeed, Miss Lyle, his landlady, had recommended it. But was it a *fashionable* church? She had not been very clear on that point. St. Peter's, the parish church, at the top of the Grand Parade, was better known, she thought, and St. Bartholomew's in Ann Street was certainly the biggest, even if the building was not to everyone's taste, but both of those were a long way to walk, and most of it uphill. St. Stephen's, after all, was just round the corner.

The notice-board outside confirmed that St. Stephen's did not cater for fashionable visitors. The list of parish activities included a blanket-lending society and a coal club. He winced and walked past, eventually catching sight of a silk hat turning down Dyke Road. It led him to West Street and St. Paul's. It was obvious, really; this was quite the most convenient venue for the socially-inclined. The King's Road, where everyone of note took carriage-exercise between the conclusion of service and luncheon, was a mere hundred yards away. The line of phaetons outside made it quite unnecessary to inspect the church notices here.

He was forced to admit, before the clergy appeared, that he was not in good shape for church-going. The organ-notes produced uncomfortable vibrations in an area at the top of his head which he had known to be sensitive this morning, but had succeeded in preserving in a quiescent state until the first blast from behind of *New Every Morning*. Saturday night at the Canterbury was about to take its toll.

He had not planned his night of gin and song. A visit to the Canterbury was not indelibly inscribed in the social diary, like evenings at the Dome and the Theatre Royal. On the contrary, it was an event one took care not to record, for it was a third-rate music hall in Church Street, on the fringe of Brighton's poor quarter, where policemen patrolled in pairs. By eight o'clock on Saturday evening it had suited his spirits better than Bernhardt in *La Dame Aux Camelias*. He had settled down with his opera-glasses among the soldiers and shop-assistants and wallowed in the banalities exchanged across the footlights, drinking steadily until the last wounds to his self-respect were rendered painless by the alcohol.

He had made his decision to have no more to do with the Protheros immediately after talking to Bridget the previous afternoon, but it took a long, brooding lunch at Booty's and a chastening march over the shingle to Black Rock to convince him that there was any point in continuing with the holiday. The experience should not have affected him so; his hobby, by its very nature, was devoted to the ephemeral, the few, fleeting seconds of clear vision before a subject moved beyond the reach of the lens. To feel deprived each time your observations were frustrated was monstrous. If he had only kept within the rules and sought nothing more than the Prussian Officer's glasses had revealed, she would still be a charming recollection, a miniature to store among the most precious in his mind's eye. Now that she was undeniably identified as a married woman and the mother of a young child, he was morally bound to dismiss her from his thoughts. He was not going to spend his holiday following other men's wives around the town. Behaviour like that was totally repugnant; it would class him with the sad-eyed squad who sat on the pebbles in front of the female bathing-machines, pretending to read *The Times*. No, dammit! He was a respectable optical instrument enthusiast. A man of science.

He turned his head slightly to take in the occupants of the pew behind, not the lady worshippers, but the men: two within view, decent, devout individuals in their Sunday suits, prayer books in hand. You would think their attention was wholly on the Second Lesson, until you watched the tiny movements of their eyes. *There* was the difference between your layman and your man of science; he had hardly registered until then that he was sitting beside one of the fair sex. Yesterday's observation of Mrs. Prothero had been in a different class altogether, a piece of scientific research. He had needed to verify the accuracy of an optical instrument

by making a closer study of the subject. That was all she was:
a legitimate subject for his researches. Much encouraged, he
stood with the congregation and joined passionately in the
singing of *Bright the vision that delighted.*

His head felt distinctly better. My, it did one good to
go to Morning Service, particularly when it clarified one's
thinking. It was all too easy for a scientist to be deflected
from the mainstream of research by secondary discoveries.
If, by some strange combination of circumstances, his
glasses chanced on the white hat again, he need feel no stir-
rings of conscience. He would clear his mind of irrelevant
associations; she meant no more to him than a butterfly
under a microscope.

As the service ended and the congregation streamed out
into dazzling sunlight, the West Pier cannon boomed. He
reached the promenade in time to see a small white cloud
disperse in an otherwise flawless sky. The gulls returned
swooping to the strips of sand exposed by the low tide.

Matins at St. Peter's must have been short, for already a
line of shining carriages was sweeping from the Old Steine
into Junction Parade at a rate suggesting they had cantered
all the way down Grand Parade. Perhaps when the vicar was
writing his sermon, he made allowance for the half-mile his
flock had to make up on the St. Paul's congregation.

He started to stroll along the King's Road in the direc-
tion of Hove, not too quickly, because he would soon reach
Preston Street, the western limit of the fashionable drive
along the front. He was in a much better frame of mind.
Brighton was quite the most exhilarating place to be this
Sunday morning. Where else could you see a sea-front so

broad that carriages could drive four-deep? And what carriages! Society was coming on parade in force, declaring its arrival in landau after landau, hauled by impeccably groomed pairs in swagger harness. Liveried coachmen in tall hats (at least two of whom he recognised from the audience at the Canterbury) sat aloft with straight backs and expressionless faces, while their passengers kept up animated conversations behind. The most resplendent carriages had their page-boys in identical livery, seated on the dickey beside the driver.

It was a field-day for the riding academies, too. Mounts of every size and breed had been hired for the morning. The strain on the resources of the stables was clear from the number of handsomely-dressed riders in the saddles of unmistakable hacks, but they scarcely detracted from the elegance of the parade.

Quite rightly the ladies took the eye, stiff-backed as guardsmen, whether mounted on saddles or carriage upholstery; a severity matched by the style of their costumes—starched collars stretching high up their necks, coats fronted with double ranks of buttons, long kid gloves—and, for the equestriennes, black riding habits, squat, shiny hats, gloved hands managing reins and crop, and a glimpse of boot-heels. The effect was mitigated in a most stimulating way by tiny outbreaks of frivolity—white lace, swansdown, ostrich feathers, the bloom of Piver's powders and the flash of kohl-washed eyes.

He was studying a team of magnificent black geldings drawing a large family phaeton, when a familiar profile crossed in front. Prothero—riding a bay. And wearing a dapper set of riding-clothes, tailor-made for certain, and a grey top hat.

The doctor's appearance in the King's Road was no surprise—where else would a professional man go after church on a Sunday morning?—and on consideration it was understandable that he was in the saddle and not with his family in a carriage. Presumably a *locum-tenens* was managing his practice and would have need of whatever form of private transport he maintained. No, what made Moscrop stand stupefied on the pavement was Dr. Prothero's patently flirtatious exchanges with a young woman riding beside him who was certainly not his wife. She was as young as Mrs. Prothero, perhaps still in her twenties, but her hair, drawn back into a chignon beneath a small black riding-hat, was a quite extraordinary shade of red, almost—was this a perverse thought?—the colour of the storm-warning cone kept on the West Pier-head. Her features were neatly proportioned, not beautiful, but lit at this moment with a radiance one could not put down alone to Brighton's bracing air.

They were past in seconds. The grate of carriage-wheels made it quite impossible to overhear their conversation. Moscrop walked on towards the Pier. Fashionable Brighton trotted past him unnoticed.

▪ On Monday it rained. He spent the morning looking at the antique shops in West Street and East Street; it was a long-standing hope of his that he would one day discover an early Venetian wooden telescope among the usual assortment of scientific bric-a-brac. He was not fortunate on this occasion, but it did provide an interesting alternative to the reading-rooms in the public and private libraries, or the humid corridors of the Aquarium, which were sure to have been well-patronised. He felt no enthusiasm for fish that morning, in spite of the attraction of a close-packed crowd of visitors.

In the afternoon he visited the roller-skating rink in West Street—a concert hall recently converted to give facilities for the newest craze. Not that he was interested in learning to skate—it looked quite as dangerous as bicycling and just as difficult to master—but he obtained a spectator's ticket and enjoyed watching less cautious spirits go through the experience. That evening he attended a concert at the Dome and found it much less diverting. His appreciation of the music ebbed away alarmingly when the thought occurred to him that he had not advanced his scientific knowledge all day.

Nor was Tuesday any more rewarding, although the sun returned and he was able to use the Zeiss from the West Pier. Repeated scannings of the beach produced not one image worth adjusting the screw-focus for. After Saturday's sighting, the number of subjects that met his criteria seemed to have diminished dramatically.

It was Wednesday morning when a routine sweep with the Zeiss of the sections of beach on the Hove side of the pier stopped abruptly on a group of bathing machines a little to the west of the Bedford Hotel. Fortunately, he was prepared for just such an occurrence. He took out the Negretti and Zambra, his most powerful portable telescope, and mounted it on a tripod, indifferent, in the way dedicated surveyors are, to the idle curiosity of passers-by. It gave him a diamond-sharp image, a positive identification that set his heart pounding with excitement. For this was a coup unequalled in his experience:

he had spotted Dr. Prothero's second son, the child Jason, sitting in his perambulator playing with a small Union Jack in front of the bathing-machines. Who else among the thousands who held telescopes to their eyes around Her Majesty's coasts would have been so observant as to recognise that tiny scrap of humanity in a sailor suit—and wearing a large white sun-hat that almost obscured his blond curls?

Curiously, young Jason appeared to be quite unaccompanied, although he was amusing himself contentedly with the flag. The beach west of the pier drew few visitors. Almost all of the Corporation's two hundred and fifty-eight machines (Moscrop had found nothing better to do the previous afternoon than count them) were concentrated in the stretch between the two piers. A few were clustered in front of the Bedford, but only the most decrepit of that hotel's guests made use of them, everyone else favouring the facilities farther along. A brief peep at the scene without the aid of the telescope showed Jason to be in sole occupation except for two couples spooning against the breakwater, and the bathing-machine attendant. The latter was a mountainous, bare-armed woman with an incipient moustache, a worthy descendant of Martha Gunn, Mrs. Fitzherbert's dipper in Regency times. As Moscrop watched, she ambled over to the child, took the slack of flesh on his cheek between the first two knuckles of her right hand and jerked his head affectionately. Jason looked surprised and stopped waving his flag.

What possible reason could there be for the child's evident abandonment on that desolate stretch of beach? Where on earth was Bridget, his nursemaid? Moscrop's sentiments plunged from triumph to acute anxiety. Could

Jason have been snatched away from his nurse and parents and deposited down there? Having sighted the child, he felt increasingly responsible for its well-being. He pulled distractedly at the ends of his moustache and beat a tattoo on the pier-deck with his left heel. With an air of decision, he dismantled the tripod, put the parts in his bag and left the pier at a quick step.

The bathing-machine woman was monstrous, quite capable of earning a second living in one of the freak shows in the arches under the promenade. When Moscrop reached her, she had taken Jason out of his pram and put him into a Corporation bath-towel which she was holding at both ends and using as a swing-boat. The child was taking the exercise manfully.

Moscrop coughed. 'You'll pardon me for asking? I think I recognise the little fellow. Is it Dr. Prothero's child?'

She stopped swinging and Jason came to rest with a springy impact against the swell of her stomach. 'What?'

'The child, Ma'am. I was inquiring if it was young Jason Prothero.'

'Couldn't tell you.' She had tiny brown eyes that seemed devoid of intelligence. 'Couldn't tell you nohow.'

'That's his pram for sure.'

She wriggled her shoulders in a non-committal way and her chins vibrated. Jason rebounded against her stomach. 'If you say so.'

'I'm certain of it.'

There was a period of silence between them with only the roll of the waves intervening.

'I see that you're looking after the boy,' he began again. 'He's in good hands.'

There was no response.

'I know something of the family, you see. It's unusual for them to be this far along the beach. Most irregular. I wonder now, would you—er—happen to have noticed who left him here?'

She took the two ends of the towel in her right hand, so that Jason was suspended inside like Baby Bunting, and pointed out to sea with the left. 'Her.'

'I beg your pardon.'

'Her. She left him here. Asked me to keep him happy.'

He climbed on the first step of the nearest bathing-machine for a better view and followed the line of her finger. There was undoubtedly someone in the water. Two people. A man and a woman bathing together. Deuced irregular. One heard that such things went on, but hardly expected to see it at Brighton in the season. Just as well they had picked one of the most isolated sections of beach.

He delved into the bag for his binoculars. Not from any indelicate motive; he merely wished to investigate a little notion that had burgeoned in his brain. The sea was choppy this morning and there was a deal of spray about. It took almost a minute's diligent work with the glasses to locate the bathers. They were holding hands, if you please, and jumping the waves together as openly as if they were fully clad and performing a *schottishe* in the Pavilion ballroom.

The man wore university costume of dark blue wool, rendered skin-tight by the water. The shoulder-straps could not have been more than two inches wide. His partner's bathing-dress of vertical red and white stripes was revealed only in glimpses, for she modestly (if such a word could be applied) endeavoured to keep her shoulders below the surface. Her hair was held in place by an oilskin mob-cap.

Then, as he watched, she was caught in the cusp of a larger wave, tipped off-balance and swept several yards inshore, shrieking in delighted panic, and ending inelegantly on hands and knees in the shallows. From there she subsided, laughing, into a sitting position, tugging down the sailor collar that had ridden up around her head. How it was that her companion was thereupon similarly upended by the action of the water and carried irresistibly towards the same spot must remain one of the ocean's mysteries. Suffice to say that the next moment Moscrop saw the red, white and blue in a conjunction that had nothing to do with patriotism. Moreover, the colours were unconscionably slow in disentangling. When at length they did, he was able, before the bathers plunged back into the deeper water with hands still linked, to confirm his earlier suspicion. The young woman in the red and white stripes was Bridget, Jason's nursemaid.

How confoundedly mistaken one can be about the fair sex! When he had helped her up the Aquarium steps with the perambulator, he had thought her a modest and responsible young woman. Yet here she was shamefully handing over the child to the mercies of this imbecilic bathing-attendant, in order to consort in the water with some inamorato from the hotel kitchens along the front.

He put down his binoculars. 'Tell me, is this assignation in the waves a regular occurrence?'

'What d'you say?' asked the fat woman.

'Have you been asked to look after the child before?'

'Oh yes. Most days. He won't come to no harm with
me. I'm not over-busy, you understand.' As if to show
how capable she was, she held Jason under his armpits and
dandled him at arms' length above her head. 'He's a nobby
little lad, don't you think?'

'I'm sure he is. Perhaps you have met his parents?' One
could not take anything for granted in the modern world.
It was always possible that Dr. Prothero knew about the
goings-on here.

'No. I just see the girl and her brother. If they bring the
young'un this way for a walk it's no hardship for me to keep
an eye on him while they enjoy themselves in the briny.'

'Her brother, you say? Are you sure of that?'

'Sure? Well, it's obvious, ain't it? He's only a lad out
there. Can't you see through them things? I hope you ain't
suggesting I'd be a party to anything improper.'

'Not at all. Not at all.' But he had already put the glasses
to his eyes to test the truth of her words.

Now that he looked more closely at Bridget's companion,
he did perceive a certain boyish leanness in the physique.
However, the antics in the spray looked most unlike the
behaviour of brother and sister. Even as he watched, an arm
crept around Bridget's waist and another lifted her at the
knees. She made a show of protesting, but allowed herself to
be carried, with some difficulty, into the shallower water.

'I don't know what it is you're being a party to, Ma'am,'
Moscrop told the bathing-machine woman, 'but I'm not
standing here to watch it any longer.'

No question of it: the youth with Bridget in his arms was
Guy Prothero.

CHAPTER 5

IN THE AFTERNOON, MOSCROP lay at full length on the shingle in front of the Grand Hotel, planning a criminal act. It began innocently enough, as an idle fancy of the sort everyone indulged in when lounging on a beach in the sun. The habit was universal; one arrived at the sea-front and marched along the promenade, searching for the most secluded spot left on the beach. Having found it and enjoyed the sensations of sun and sea for a few minutes, one began looking to right and left and taking a mild inter-est in the neighbours one had sought so conscientiously to keep at a distance: the man who had removed his shoes and socks; the young woman with the bad-tempered dog; the couple complaining loudly about their hotel. As the day progressed it was natural enough to speculate on the kinds of lives such people led. How did a man like that behave in his own home; what monstrous lapses of decorum did his family have to endure? Whatever attracted a woman as pretty as she to a dog like that; did she have no friends at all? What class of hotel would satisfy those people; did they live to such exalted standards? It was a short step from that stage to the next: the occasion for contact. It arose from any trivial occurrence: the hat or parasol caught in a sudden gust and blown along the beach; the runaway terrier; the wasp-sting requiring instant attention from the blue-bag one had providently packed. From there the association prospered or perished, according to taste. But there was no denying that a public beach provided more scope for studying one's fellow-beings and more opportunities for broadening one's acquaintance than anywhere else except a hospital ward.

To put the facts correctly, Moscrop's neighbours on Brighton beach were not entirely unknown to him. In his case, there was no need for speculation about their identity: they were Mrs. Prothero, Guy, young Jason and Bridget. He had tracked them to this spot with the tenacity of a border scout, even suffering himself to lunch on cockles from a stall below the pier, while Guy, Bridget and the child took lunch from a hamper. Mrs. Prothero had joined them here soon after two; the Doctor was not with her. And now Moscrop lay some thirty yards to their rear, flouting the principles on which he had based the whole of his researches.

He despised himself for it. Even the act of lying here, trying not to jump like a grasshopper each time one of them moved, was a surrender. Observation held no joys now; it was a furtive, skulking business, undignified by any connection with scientific practice. He had no choice, though. He had ceased to be a scientist the moment the white hat had

danced across his lens. The last two days with his instruments had convinced him of that. Binocular-work for its
own sake was now a barren occupation.

Strange how each discovery about the members of
the family, however odious, had nourished his curiosity
about Mrs. Prothero. She sat half-turned away from
him now, flanked by Guy and Bridget, leaning her back
against an upturned fishing-smack. Down at the water,
a small pleasure-boat was taking on passengers and she
was watching it, amused at the efforts of the ladies not
to overbalance on the narrow plank bridging the foam.
The hat, the same hat, responded to the tremors of her
body, as she tried not to giggle openly. One unexpected
sea breeze was all that was wanted to lift it off her head for
him to retrieve. One small gust between himself and an
introduction.

He was not prepared to wait for it. Why, he might still
be there in suspense at the end of the afternoon, when they
got up to leave. It was no use waiting for an act of God, like
that; better, surely, to improvise your own.

He looked around him. The situation was promising. Few
people had chosen to sit as high up the beach as he. A couple
to his right were totally absorbed in each other. Several of an
older generation were dozing in the sunshine. The bathing-
machines to the rear were unoccupied.

The pleasure-boat filled up and cast off. Mrs. Prothero
returned to a novel she was reading. Guy was aiming pebbles
into Jason's tin bucket, mounted on a heap of stones ahead
of him. Bridget was knitting. The child was quite content to
circle the boat, one small hand on the upturned hull to assist

its balance. From the right, a minstrel band was progressing up the beach with banjo, bones and harmonium.

With the casual air of a practised criminal, Moscrop got to his feet, walked to within fifteen yards of the boat and sat down again. This was one occasion when he could have done without his bag, but he was not to have known that earlier. He opened it and looked inside. It might have its uses, even so. He took out the Negretti and Zambra.

Young Jason was completing his fourth or fifth wobbly circumambulation of the boat. As he toddled round the prow, out of sight of his family, his attention was diverted by a sudden snapping sound. Moscrop had pulled the telescope open to its full extent and then closed it. The child paused. Moscrop smiled, and repeated the action. Farther down the beach, the black-faced minstrels were catching everyone's eye.

He held out the telescope. It flashed in the sunlight. Jason left the support of the boat and started towards it. One of the black-faced singers was approaching Mrs. Prothero with hat extended, jingling the coins inside. Behind her, Jason reached out for the telescope. Moscrop smiled, pulled it open, snapped it shut, stood up, and started walking slowly off the beach, dangling the instrument tantalisingly in his right hand. Jason paused, glanced momentarily behind him, and then started after the new toy. The minstrels were ranged in front of Mrs. Prothero, serenading her.

Behind the bathing-machines, he replaced the telescope in his Gladstone bag, pausing as if undecided whether to leave the beach. A second later, a small, flaxen-curled infant came round the side. Moscrop bent down. 'Hello, hello, little man. And where would you be going? To buy some barley sugar, no doubt. We'll go that way together.' When Jason looked doubtful about the proposition, the telescope was miraculously planted in his hands. Moscrop held one end and Jason the other. The sweet-shop was one of a row built into the arches under the promenade. The others sold fresh fish, fruit and baskets coated with shells. There was a wooden seat just within the arch, out of sight of the beach. He helped Jason on to it and gave him a stick of barley sugar.

The abduction—or, rather, enticement—lasted about fifteen minutes, by which time the barley sugar had rolled under the seat, the telescope, coated with sticky fingerprints, was replaced in the bag and Jason was bawling more loudly than the fishwife next door. Moscrop purchased a stick of liquorice, which might conceivably have resembled a telescope, offered it, had it rejected, stuffed it in his pocket, snatched up child and bag and started back across the pebbles towards the upturned boat.

Bridget was standing alone, biting her finger-nails in anguish. When she saw Moscrop approaching, she stumbled across the shingle to meet him. 'Oh sir, you've brought him back to me safe! Let me take him. Mistress is out of her mind with worry. She's down by the water there, looking for him. We thought he was drowned, for sure!'

'I recognised you from Saturday afternoon,' he explained, to make his sudden arrival quite clear.

'Why, of course! The gentleman who helped me up the stairs! Oh, Mistress will be so grateful. We must wave to her.'

They waved. Mrs. Prothero saw them, clutched her hand to her forehead and waved back. It was one of the finest moments of Moscrop's life.

'I don't know how we should have told the master,' said Bridget. 'Guy went off—Master Guy, that is—to see if them black-faced men had kidnapped him.'

Mrs. Prothero was coming quickly up the beach. Moscrop took the liquorice from his pocket, pushed it into Jason's hand and curled the little fingers firmly over it. 'We passed a sweet-shop,' he explained to Bridget with a shy smile.

'How very kind! Oh, Mrs. Prothero, Ma'am, there you are. This gentleman has brought Jason back safe, with not one curl of his little head harmed, and bought him sweets as well!'

'Albert Moscrop, Ma'am. It was nothing at all.'

'Nothing?' She stood a yard from him, fixing him unexpectedly with a ferocious pout from under the hat. 'You can't mean it. Jason Prothero lost without trace, his Ma in a state of advanced hysteria, the beach about to be turned over stone by stone and you arrive from nowhere with the child in your arms and describe it as nothing! He's a wilful little beast, I grant you. Call him what you like, my dear, but don't hand him back to his demented mother like a dropped handkerchief.'

Her voice was pitched low, the words exquisitely mouthed, and all the more devastating for that.

He fumbled for a response. 'On the contrary, Ma'am. A beautiful child. I . . .

'Good God!' she said. 'I've offended the man. I'm the most tactless woman alive, Mr. . . . Mr. . . .

'Moscrop, Ma'am.'

'A name to remember. Understand that I'm most awfully grateful. Words cannot suffice. I was on the brink of despair. A desperate woman, Mr. . . . what did you say it was, darling?'

'Moscrop.' This was so unlike the scene he had visualised. He groped back to his prepared speech. 'It was providential that I recognised your servant, Ma'am. I gave her a helping hand when she was trying to negotiate the Aquarium steps with a pram the other afternoon. If I hadn't seen her just now, I'd have taken the little fellow to the police station. The law takes its time, I believe. You might have presumed the worst by now.'

'Darling,' (she used the endearment in a way that made him feel on a par with Jason), 'as far as I was concerned he was already food for the fishes. Where on earth did you find the brat?'

'You see the groyne up there towards the pier?'

'God, he didn't get that far?'

'I found him taking a walk along the top, Ma'am. He must have climbed up where the stones are heaped against it, near the water's edge.'

'On the *top!* Suppose he had fallen!'

'He might have escaped with a bruise or two on *this* side, Ma'am, but if he'd fallen the other way there's a ten foot drop. At the point where I caught up with him, that is.'

She cradled Jason to her bosom, reckless of liquorice stains. 'You saved his life, by Heaven! You saved my son's life. The gentleman's a hero, Bridget, a saint, and you, my girl, are the other thing. What were you doing to let my child wander off and all but kill himself? Dr. Prothero shall hear of this. Go and find Guy this minute and tell him what has happened. Then return with him at once.'

A film of tears spread over Bridget's eyes. She turned and stumbled along the stones in the direction the minstrels had taken. Moscrop felt a pang of sympathy for the girl, which quite dispersed when he realised her departure left him alone with Mrs. Prothero. Except, of course for Jason.

'Shall we sit down a moment, Mr. Moscrop?' The voice had a carriage-wheel quality, a rich, grating resonance that made the most simple suggestion sound like an invitation to unexampled intimacies. 'You must wait and meet my stepson. But I have the advantage of you. My name is Prothero. Zena Prothero.'

She held out her gloved hand. Oh the contact! The touch of her palm through the lace snuffed out a lifetime's devotion to optical research. From that moment the bagful of instruments at his feet was obsolete.

She lowered herself confidently to the stones and arranged her dress. Moscrop stood by uncertainly. Much as he desired it, he could not openly sit beside her with his back against the boat. It was, after all, a public beach. He compromised by removing the telescope from his bag, crouching to give it to Jason and then remaining in that position.

Heavens, yes, peering through a lens couldn't be compared to this. Now that he had seen her at close quarters, heard her speak, actually touched her, he realised how different she was from all other women. Conversing with her was not easy; she said such unpredictable things, quite unlike the things he was used to women saying, all those women he had observed by the hour at the fashionable south coast resorts. Well to be quite accurate about it he had not been near enough to overhear any of their conversations, but he *knew* how they talked, the tones of their voices, the silly, trivial, engaging things they said. It never varied, from

Torquay to Broadstairs. From the narrow end of a pair of binoculars, they all talked and behaved exactly like his sister Maud; so had Zena Prothero, until this confrontation.

'Are you a resident of Brighton, Ma'am?'

'No, my dear, more's the pity. Gregory has a practice in Dorking, and we've escaped for three weeks. We are staying at the Albemarle. Comfortable, but monstrously expensive. You are here for the season, I expect.'

'Just three weeks, like you,' said Moscrop. 'I'm one of those deplorable individuals who cannot bear to be away from their business for more than the minimum. It betrays a lack of confidence, I'm afraid.'

'Oh skittles, darling! You're conscientious, like Prothero. He's a doctor—did I tell you? Do you know that he has already given up four or five days of his holiday to visit former patients, retired people who moved here for reasons of health?'

He tried to appear impressed, but he could not forget the red-headed equestrienne. *She* had looked some way short of retirement. 'Admirable, Ma'am. I've always held that it's a capital doctor who still takes an interest in a former patient. There'll be plenty for him to visit here, I'm sure. It's a favourite spot for the convalescent, I've heard, what with its ozone and its chalybeate water.'

'He's visiting a poor old soul in Rottingdean this very afternoon, dear. Otherwise he'd be here with us. There's dedication for you! Between ourselves, though, he doesn't care very much for the sea-shore. He rather disapproves when I bring the children on the beach. It's not the *thing* in the season, is it? I find the sea irresistible, though. There, that's my lower class origins revealed! Now I can see from the way *you're* crouching that you aren't in your element, darling.'

'Oh, on the contrary, I . . .'

'Sit on the stones, my dear. Give your legs a rest. The shingle's cleaner than you think. Now tell me all about Jason's misadventure. Where were you when you spotted him—on the prom?'

'Oh. That is—er—yes.' The conversation was drifting into dangerous straits. 'May I ask you a question, Mrs. Prothero?'

'Anything you like, my dear—provided Prothero wouldn't disapprove.'

Heavens! What did she expect? 'Do you always favour this part of the beach?'

She laughed for no evident reason. 'Why yes. It is altogether convenient. Guy likes to bathe from the machines near the pier there, Jason has his Punch and Judy show and I adore watching the excursion-yachts. Ah, Bridget has found Guy—the only useful thing that madam has done today.' She waved to her stepson. He had come by way of the sand at the water's edge, for ease of walking. Bridget trotted after him superfluously.

'A fine-looking lad. There's an upright look about him,' said Moscrop, as though he meant it.

'D'you think so, darling?' (he fervidly hoped she would drop the endearment when Guy joined them). 'He is not the easiest boy in the world to manage. It must be beastly for him to have to accept me as his stepmother.'

The cue for a compliment. 'Quite the contrary, Ma'am. He could not possibly find anyone more acceptable.

His difficulty, I suggest, is that you are far too *chic* to be thought of in a maternal capacity.'

Guy approached with hand extended. Not before Moscrop had seen Zena Prothero blush. Such timing! He stood to meet the boy with the casual air of Irving after some brilliantly-delivered line on the stage of the Lyceum.

'Guy Prothero. I understand you saved my stepbrother's life, sir.'

'I wouldn't put it as strongly as that. Simply returned him to his mother.'

'We're grateful, even so. Give me your card and I'll inform my father. He'll wish to show his appreciation. D'you smoke cigars?'

Damned impudence! 'That won't be necessary.' He addressed himself to Zena: 'Now that your stepson has returned, I'll take my leave, Ma'am. If I might just recover the telescope from young Jason . . .'

She had given Guy a thunderous look. 'You can't leave like this. I shan't allow it. You must have dinner with us at the very least. Where are you staying, Mr. Moscrop?'

He touched his bowler in as decisive a parting gesture as he could devise. 'Most generous of you, Mrs. Prothero, but I really couldn't put you to so much trouble. Your husband is a busy man—'

'Fudge! If he's too busy to meet the hero who saved his son's life, I want to know the reason why!'

Guy said something in an aside to Bridget.

'What was that?' demanded Mrs. Prothero.

'We should leave it to Father to make the arrangements. Do you carry cards, Mr. . . . ? But perhaps your name is published in the *Fashionable Visitors' List?'* The note of sarcasm was blatantly calculated to insult.

'Guy! Kindly leave this to me! Take Jason down to the water with Bridget and clean his hands and face.'

The boy shrugged, took a long look at Moscrop, felt in his blazer-pocket for his snuff-box, sniffed some gracelessly, continuing to stare, replaced the box, nodded to Bridget (who picked up Jason), turned and walked slowly away, kicking at pebbles as he went.

'Your telescope, Mr. Moscrop.' She held it out and as quickly withdrew it. 'Oh, but it wants cleaning. The liquorice.'

'Not with your handkerchief, Ma'am. It is far too delicate to soil.' But she was already at work, diligently rubbing the chromium. She might have been scrubbing his back, it gave him so much pleasure.

'You understand my problem now,' she said as she worked. 'I must apologise for the boy's behaviour.'

'Not at all. A difficult age, Ma'am. A difficult age.'

'Darling, if you only knew how difficult . . . This is a beautiful instrument, Mr. Moscrop. You shouldn't have given it to Jason to play with. Lord, I hope the lenses are not damaged! May I look through it?'

'But of course.' He stood against the boat, ready to assist.

'I shall try to pick out Jason. Is he too near for focusing? My dear, I can't see anything at all.'

Surely this was an invitation! He knelt beside her as she peered through the eye-piece and put his right hand gently over hers to adjust the focus. 'Hold the telescope steady, then. As I draw out the tube the image will form and you can make it sharper by small adjustments. Do you see any-thing yet? I am extending it slowly so that you can tell me.' And so that she could feel the gentle pressure of his fingers on hers.

'Oh yes! Don't move it any more, darling. Perfect!' she said. 'I can see Bridget as clear as you like, wretched girl. Ah! There is Jason with his feet in the water. What a powerful instrument, Mr. Moscrop!' She handed it back to him.

'It's built for longer distances, actually. If there were a steam-boat in sight . . . I'd better put it away, however. My hobby, you know. Optical instruments. My profession, in fact. I have a shop in Oxford Street.'

'In London? How exciting! Now I know why you cannot bear to be away for more than three weeks at a time. Darling, you *must* meet my husband. Gregory would be fascinated with your hobby. He has two microscopes himself which I polish for him sometimes. You and he would have so much in common.'

Moscrop got to his feet, picking up his bag. 'I hope you'll forgive me for saying so, Mrs. Prothero. It's been a rare pleasure talking with you. One never knows what will happen on a beach, does one? It would be an honour to meet Dr. Prothero, and I'm sure he would make me most welcome, but I feel that this afternoon began on the beach with young Jason—and ought to end there. It was a small thing I did, Ma'am. Isn't it best in the circumstances not to mention it to the doctor? A thing like that's sure to discom-mode a man, somewhat. Might lead to the devil of a scene with your servant. I wouldn't want that to spoil your holiday. Besides, he might be so worried about Jason's safety that he stopped you from coming to the beach. Then, forgive me, I shouldn't have the possibility of passing the time of day with you if I came for a walk along the seashore.'

She smiled. It had been a lengthy explanation. 'Very well, my dear. You are too persuasive. I shall instruct Guy to say nothing. He likes Bridget, I suspect, and will cooperate. But I shall not forget your kindness.'

CHAPTER 6

THERE WAS A DISTURBANCE on the surface of the water in Brill's Gentlemen's Swimming Bath—the First Class Bath—in East Street. A head bobbed above water-level, fairish hair flattened to it, revealing unmistakable signs of baldness at the crown: Albert Moscrop's. He trod water for a few seconds, rearranging his moustache. Behind him two other swimmers performed stately breast-strokes across different diameters of the circular pool. It was sixty-five feet across, the largest of its kind in Europe. Visitors cognisant of the health-giving effects of manly exercises patronised Brill's First Class Bath as devotedly in the season as the philharmonic concerts at the Pavilion.

Inhaling deeply to inflate his lungs, he inclined his head backwards and allowed body and legs to swing from the vertical to the horizontal so that two sets of white toes broke the surface ahead of him. First-rate water for floating: sea-water obtained, as the management were at pains to point out in a notice in the foyer (in view of recent disclosures in *The Lancet*), from Cliftonville. He relaxed in this supine position, exercising his mind on the meaning of the Latin inscription around the walls; giving that up and looking at the gallery, empty today, but with seating for 400 spectators; finally putting his head right back in the water and enjoying the beauty of Sir Giles Gilbert Scott's domed ceiling. All so congenial that he wished he could credit himself with the idea of coming here.

The proper cause of his visit was seated on the tiled perimeter of the pool with feet dangling in the water, testing its temperature and trying to appear casual about it—Gregory Prothero, M.D., in stripes worthy of a Hokey Pokey cart.

Moscrop's conversation with Mrs. Prothero on the beach the previous afternoon had been a revelation. His first reaction had been one of shock, she was so unlike the personality he had assigned to her when he watched her through the binoculars. He had automatically classed her with the numerous sweet, shy and submissive young women catalogued in his memory from hours of observation of seaside promenades and beaches. Yet there she was, as exquisite as any of them, in a single breath invoking the Deity, castigating a domestic and addressing a total stranger in terms of intimate endearment. If his legs had not lost all mobility he would certainly have turned and fled. How could a vision of such elegance and refinement come to possess a turn of phrase like that?

The devil of it was that as the first shock receded he had

found himself increasingly fascinated by the gravelly voice assaulting his sensibilities. The perfect consonants and immaculate vowel-sounds gently teased him into a state of acceptance. Before the conversation ended he was snatching up the familiarities like dropped coins. The character he had given her in his imagination was quite displaced and so, if he admitted it, were the characters of all the winsome subjects of his observations. If she was so different on acquaintance, why not they? There was nothing else for it but to renounce the achromatic lens for ever.

For all the strength of her invective she was disturbingly vulnerable. Jason's adventure, by her own admission, had driven her to the brink of despair. Guy appeared to hold her in total contempt. As for her husband. . . . One did not want to jump to conclusions. Perhaps she was justified in accepting Prothero's word that when he left her to spend the day alone it was because he was visiting former patients. Perhaps the red-headed young woman riding beside him in the King's Road parade was known to her only in a medical capacity. Tea-rose complexion and flashing eyes notwith-standing, she might well be recuperating from some debility discernible only to a medical man. It was also conceivable that the lady harpist in the Aquarium Orchestra was a convalescent whose condition was a matter of professional concern to Dr. Prothero. In matters as delicate as this one was well-advised to preserve an open mind for as long as practicable. Nevertheless, the possibility existed that an innocent and trusting woman was being deceived. Without committing himself any further, Moscrop had resolved to watch Dr. Prothero very closely indeed.

For all that, it was a matter for self-congratulation that he was watching him from his present position. A lesser man might have baulked at the door of Brill's, particularly when arriving there without a costume. It took considerable *savoir-faire* in such circumstances to arrange with the attendant for the hire of the requisite garment. He had followed Prothero there from the forecourt of the Albemarle Hotel, which he had now taken in as part of his morning constitutional—the major part, in fact, for he had passed three-quarters of an hour patrolling it, before the doctor's appearance soon after eleven. He had then discreetly pursued his quarry along the front, in some anticipation of witnessing an assignation.

But at East Street Prothero had turned in to Brill's. And although the sign *Ladies' and Gentlemen's First and Second-Class Swimming Baths* caused Moscrop a flutter of expectation, it was subdued at once by the discovery that there were separate entrances for the sexes. Mixed bathing was strictly confined to the more remote stretches of the beach. Brill's Gentlemen's section, he soon discovered, was not unlike a club, with its uniformed staff, lounges, reading- and billiards-rooms. There were also the two main pools, a vapour bath, a medical douche and a barber's shop. If anything untoward happened here, it was not a clandestine meeting between a gentleman and a lady.

So he had paid his one shilling and sixpence, picked up his borrowed costume—'every one freshly laundered after each hiring, sir,' he was assured—and followed the doctor's top hat through the steam to the First Class pool. There, with a touch of brilliance, he had let himself unnoticed into a cubicle on the side opposite, stripped as if his life depended on it, put on the costume and jumped into the water before the doctor unbolted his door. Even as he surfaced, a pair of still-stockinged feet were visible through the gap under Prothero's door. Who would suspect as he entered a swimming bath that a bather already immersed had followed him there?

What he had not allowed for in his inspired rush to the water was the scarcity of swimmers. He was only the third to take the plunge. Between leaving *terra firma* and making his first contact with *aqua marina* he suffered an instant's apprehension that the water-temperature might be the reason, but he was reassured. It was pleasantly tepid. Doubtless like most social institutions, Brill's was heavily patronised at certain times and deserted by all but a few enthusiasts at others.

Prothero was patently in no hurry to swim. He had appeared from his cubicle some three minutes after Moscrop's immersion and remained by the door, limbering up with toe-touching and knee-bending exercises, an exasperating little man, spry in movement and trim in figure. If anything, he appeared younger out of his clothes than in them. Moscrop wondered as he watched from the pool whether a reassessment of the doctor's age was in order, bald head or no. It was easy to understand a man in such fine physical shape having a certain attraction to the fair sex. Not at all surprising that he should have married three times. Why, it was not beyond the bounds of possibility that he should. . . . Good Lord! Was this keeping an open mind? To discipline his thinking, Moscrop put thumb and forefinger to his nostrils and dipped his head under the water. When he surfaced, the doctor was sitting at the edge with legs neatly crossed.

'How's the water?'

The words literally went over his head as he floated there. He was not used to conversations interrupting his vigils. Observation was essentially a silent occupation. He was still making a mental estimate of the positions of the other two swimmers to ascertain which one Prothero was addressing when the question was repeated.

'I said how's the water?'

No doubt about it. The doctor was speaking to him. Deuced awkward. This wasn't at all a part of his strategy. What could he do—ignore the fellow? Pretend he hadn't heard? It might have worked if the bath had been swarming with swimmers, but this morning it really wouldn't do. He lifted his head and his eyes met Prothero's.

'Thought you were wearing ear-plugs for a moment. Is it cold this morning?'

Small-talk. Best to go through the formalities and then swim out of earshot at the first opportunity. 'Not excessively.'

'I believe in accustoming the body to the water gradually,' Prothero explained. 'There's no benefit in sudden shocks to the system.'

Was this his way of saying he had observed the splash in the pool a few minutes before?

'Mind you,' the doctor went on, 'once I'm in the water I don't believe in paddling about. Oh no, it's important not to catch cold. Used in the right way, sea-water's the finest balm a doctor can prescribe, did you know that? Marvellous for scrofulous infections.'

'Really?'

'Oh yes, indeed. All forms of paralysis, nervous afflictions, hysteria, headaches, indigestion. Nothing like sea-water to cure 'em. I wouldn't recommend bathing from a public beach, mind.'

'No?'

'By God, no! Contaminated water. The stuff you're lying in is pumped from Cliftonville, or I shouldn't have my feet in it, I can tell you. I've no liking for open-air bathing, anyway. Did my share of it as a young man, you know, but that was when a fellow wasn't ashamed to swim in the buff.

'Here for the season, are you?'

'Er—yes.'

'Me, too. I never miss it. There was one year when I was here from race-week to Christmas and I don't think I missed more than half-a-dozen balls all season. That was a long time back, though. I've buried two wives since then and acquired a third.'

Moscrop was not sure whether to offer condolences or congratulations. The doctor was not waiting for responses, anyway.

'Emily died of smallpox. Solicitor's daughter with a good dowry. Set me up in practice. Stella was my second. One of the Pelhams. D'you know 'em? Landed family. She ate some bad fish. Killed her overnight. You can see why I'm so strong on contamination.'

'By Jove, yes. But you married again?'

'My third?' Prothero sniffed. 'Yes. Went for good looks this time. Married a bit beneath my station. Shop-keeper's daughter. Easy on the eye, but a bit of a liability on social occasions.' He got to his feet. 'Time I got my costume wet, I think.' He entered the water with an agile header and struck out powerfully for the opposite side, using the new Trudgeon stroke. It would not be wise to under-estimate Dr. Prothero.

Moscrop contrived to keep well clear of his new acquaintance, employing the more conventional side-stroke to cross the pool at a different angle. It was as well that he had the physical exercise to occupy him, for he was shaking with indignation, outraged by Prothero's contemptuous description of the woman he was privileged to call his wife. To say that Zena—from now on, he refused to think of Prothero's name in association with hers—was 'easy on the eye' was like calling the Crystal Palace a glass-house. The man was boorish and insensitive, totally unworthy of her. And, what worried Moscrop more, he had admitted to regarding her as a 'liability'; what on earth did that mean?

After four diameters, Prothero left the pool by putting his hands on the side and jumping out with a neat bunny-hop. 'Don't believe in staying in the water longer than necessary, you know,' he called. 'Danger of chills. I'm going to take off my costume and give myself a good rubbing with a coarse towel. Get the body glowing, what?'

Moscrop waited for the sound of the bolt being turned in the door of Prothero's cubicle before clambering out by way of the steps and locating his own clothes. For him, the process of towelling was necessarily brief; he needed to be ready to take up the pursuit as soon as the doctor quitted his cubicle. From now on, he would be exercising his wits to the full to avoid detection. It was no good bemoaning his lost anonymity. He should count himself lucky that only his face had been revealed; the doctor had no idea what height he was or what clothes he wore. Thank Heavens for a bowler and flannels!

By standing on the seat inside his cubicle he was able to watch the locked door across the pool for the sure indication that it was about to be unbolted—the sight of the crown of a silk hat above it. When it appeared, he ducked out of sight, counted up to twenty and set off after the doctor. In the steam-filled corridor outside, he almost caught him up, but had the resource to stop at a mangle and put his wet costume through it. In the foyer he paused again to return it to the attendant. By then his quarry was outside and crossing East Street. He followed him warily, down to the front, turning right into the King's Road. The cannon on the West Pier fired. The doctor did what scores of other men were doing at that moment: checked his watch. Then he moved on to the eastern corner of West Street and marched through a dark green painted doorway and out of sight. Moscrop hurried towards it to read the legend over the door, *Real Turtle Soup Always Ready*. Dr. Prothero was dining at Mutton's.

The aroma issuing from the double glass door all but seduced Moscrop inside. Turtle soup exerted a strong pull on a stomach subsisting on a Brighton landlady's cold beef and bread puddings. Moreover, he already had it in mind to patronise Mutton's; wasn't it one of Brighton's institutions, the logical place to visit after a bathe? Not while Dr. Prothero was inside, he decided with admirable self-control. His bowl of real turtle soup was the sacrifice he had to make to preserve what was left of his incognito. So he made a purchase at Streeter's, the old bun-shop in Pool Valley, and dined surreptitiously from a paper bag, endeavouring to watch the entrance to Mutton's from a position on the promenade where he could appear to be feeding seagulls.

Prothero must have had a second bowl and perhaps a third, for it was almost two o'clock when he appeared again. He set off along the front on the shop side of the street, retracing his steps towards Brill's, past the Old Ship and the pungent hop-smells of Black Lion Street. At East Street, Brighton's most fashionable row of shops, he turned left. Window-displays of wigs, china and antiques, artfully arranged to catch the seasonable visitor's eye, left him unmoved; he walked with the resolute step of a man with somewhere to go. This proved to be the French chocolate shop halfway up the hill. He marched straight in and presently came out carrying a box tied with a ribbon.

Chocolates. He had bought some chocolates for his wife.

Moscrop, watching discreetly through festoons of lace in the window of Chillmaid and Tinkler, felt something sinister stirring in the recesses of his mind. A macabre association. Chocolates . . . and Brighton. What on earth was it? Something to do with *Punch*, or one of the humorous journals. Three or four years ago, it must have been. Chocolate . . . ah! Chocolate creams! The case of Christiana Edmunds, that wrong-headed young woman who had injected chocolate-creams with strychnine. She had returned them to a Brighton shop vainly expecting that the man she secretly loved would buy them for his wife. A child of four had consumed one and died. The press—he remembered clearly now—joked after the conviction that it was now easier to sell ice-creams to Esquimaux than chocolate-creams in Brighton. Appalling case. Good gracious, how one's mind wandered!

Prothero re-passed the shop, heading towards the King's Road again. The benevolent look in his eye struck deep into Moscrop's conscience. Dammit, the man was taking chocolates to his wife. To connect that laudable action with the sordid circumstances of a murder case was unforgivable. Outrageous.

When Prothero reached the front he crossed the road and approached one of the penny-a-peep men at the promenade railing. What could he want with a telescope? The *Brighton* was not due to sail for another hour and there was not a decent-sized vessel in sight. He seemed to know what he was about, though; swung the thing straight round and focused it along the water's edge in a westerly direction. Was it the water he was watching, or the beach itself? Yes, by Jove, he had it trained on a stretch of shingle somewhere in front of the Grand. The very spot where Zena liked to sit. But of course! He was planning to surprise his young wife with the chocolates. He was making quite sure that she was there.

Moscrop looked away, his whole impression of Dr. Prothero thrown in doubt. What more touching testimony to conjugal love was there than the spectacle of this middle-aged man clutching his chocolates and seeking out his wife?

It was as well that he looked again, for when Prothero had taken his pennyworth at the telescope he turned about and set off at a stroll in precisely the opposite direction from where Zena was. The bounder made off along Junction Parade as if he had no ties at all. At the clock-tower over the Aquariam entrance, he checked his watch again. It was not the automatic gesture a man on a walk might make;

he actually stopped, produced a pair of *pince-nez* from one pocket and the watch from another, stared hard at the clock, waiting, and, when the large hand made its small movement to the twentieth minute, he lifted his own time-piece in front of his face, like a chemist studying events in a test-tube. Then, without making any adjustment, he pocketed watch and glasses and moved on. Either he was in possession of a suspect watch or there was some rendezvous he was most conscientious about keeping.

Moscrop followed at a strategic distance, hands clasped behind his back, eyes ranging convincingly to left and right, professing strong interest in a goat-chaise or pleasure-yacht or whatever came within his purview. There was small chance yet of the doctor spotting him if he turned round, but he was using this more populated stretch to practise a convincing afternoon stroll. The esplanades beyond the Chain Pier were disturbingly less frequented.

Sensibly, he refused to countenance feelings of guilt about what he was doing. It was his privilege to spend his holiday in whatever way he chose. If other people preferred to wander aimlessly along the promenades or sit bemused on the beach they were perfectly entitled so to do. He had always maintained that his optical experiments were merely a more purposeful way of enjoying the bounties of the seashore, the intelligent man's style of vacation. And his innovations this year were a logical extension of those experiments. The previous holidays, whether at Eastbourne or Folkestone or Worthing, had all, on reflection, been somewhat sedentary in character. This year he was getting exercise as well as ozone.

The afternoon was splendid for walking: a bright, clear sky; the sea full of interest, flecked with white; the tamarisk on the slopes below the Madeira Drive stirred by a soft sea-breeze. Dr. Prothero walked with the air of a man intent on savouring the balmy atmosphere to the full, rakishly raising his hat to ladies reclining on hotel balconies or in the backs of phaetons, ruffling the hair of a child who came within range and stopping to take a long proprietorial look at the Royal Crescent. For his pursuer, this uneven progress was more than a little trying, particularly when the last of the shops was passed and there were so few pedestrians that everyone took an interest in everyone else. He kept some fifty yards behind, taking the sea-wall side of the Marine Parade, although it afforded less cover, simply because it would have been con-spicuous to have taken the other. After the fashion of apart-ment-letting localities, the street-doors were left open as if to invite inspection, so unless you were seeking accommodation you used the sea-wall side. Although this saved him from the serious scrutiny of landladies, it made him the cynosure of the bow window and balcony set, so it was essential to present the appearance of a casual stroller.

After more than a mile, the broad lawns fronting on Lewes Crescent interrupted the line of terraces. Here Prothero paused, as he had at the Royal Crescent and Marine Square, and took stock of the architecture. Moscrop, alive to every shift of the chase, descended some convenient steps and seated himself on the sloping lawn between Marine Parade and the lower esplanade. It was an inspired manoeuvre, for Prothero, fifty yards ahead, found a similar row of steps and began to move purposefully down the slope towards one of the several alcoves built into the sloping cliff wall. It was set out with a table and seats. He stood beside the table and examined his watch. Moscrop did the same. Two minutes to three.

Next he witnessed a spectacle that made him inclined to believe, even in that brilliant afternoon sunshine, that he was watching some psychic manifestation. Below him and to his left, but above the alcove, were two humble cottages, gardeners' dwellings, he would guess. From between these, as if at a signal, there emerged a procession of five women in black dresses. They wore aprons and white hats and carried trays of silver tea-pots and cups and saucers and plates, which they presently arranged on the table. Then they withdrew without a word and disappeared between the hovels as uncannily as they had arrived.

The apparitions were not finished yet. From the same spot glided a young woman in a gown of some exquisitely fine material, percale or camlet, in peacock blue, and carrying a matching parasol. Prothero rose to meet her and kissed her hand. Then he presented her with the chocolates. As she looked down to examine them, part of her hair was momentarily freed from the parasol's shadow. It glowed a copper colour. She was Prothero's riding-companion of the King's Road parade.

He watched them for more than an hour. Impossible to hear what they were saying, but their expressions, their gestures told everything. When they got up to leave, she took his arm as if it were the most natural thing in the world. They walked up the slope linked, as brazenly as that.

He was so absorbed in this monstrous infidelity that he quite failed to realise the way they were taking. Only when they had passed between the cottages and disappeared did he descend the slope to examine the place for himself. As he got there, the line of servant-women passed him on their way to retrieve the tea-things, stone-faced as only the best-trained domestics are. But if they revealed nothing, at least the secret of their miraculous appearances was laid bare: the arched entrance to a subterranean tunnel, through which Prothero and his companion had undoubtedly passed. A passage under the Marine Parade to the private gardens of Lewes Crescent.

CHAPTER 7

FROM NORTH STREET, WHERE the next day's observations
had led him, Moscrop heard the boom of the mid-day cannon. He kept his hands stubbornly away from his watch-
chain. The curious thing about an annual summer holiday
was that one spent the rest of the year looking forward to
the escape it would provide from the daily round of breakfast, cab, business, lunch, business, cab, dinner, bed—and
promptly surrendered to a routine just as rigid, reinforced
by a pier cannon and a landlady's gong. By the end of the
first week one was telling the days by the menu. Quite innocent events, the first chord of the lunch-hour concert, or the
hoot of the steamship *Brighton*, took on an awful, inexorable
sameness. It was impossible not to count the days already
gone and, with increasing agitation, the few left. Harassed
visitors in their second week could be observed wading out
determinedly into the unfriendliest of seas. The ultimate

defeat was the visit to the promenade photographer to set the holiday on record; by then one was mentally already back in London.

His own case was not quite like that. The pressures he felt were not to be resolved in some shabby photographic studio. It seemed to him that a situation of tragic proportions was being revealed to him. There was nothing he could do to intervene. He had to submit to its inevitability, watch it progress in its own time, like the tide. Each contact with the Protheros laid bare a fresh layer of deceit, the deceit being practised on an innocent woman by everyone around her, husband, son, servant. If anything could be depended upon, it was that Zena Prothero's pathetically misplaced trust would soon be shattered. The prospect was hideous, unspeakable, too awful to contemplate, and he could do nothing but watch and wait.

At this moment she was admiring North Street's window-show with her two sons, Guy and Jason, and the maid, Bridget, the four of them idling along the pavements towards East Street, stopping frequently and remarking on things that caught their attention, the very image of family harmony. In a lemon-coloured gown, sealskin jacket and black bonnet, she looked particularly frail this morning. Oh for the reassurance of her robust style of conversation!

Obviously they would turn into East Street and make their way down to the front, so with a touch of brilliance he got ahead of them on the other side of the street, turned the corner, walked some fifty yards and stepped out of sight into a shop entrance. Not by chance had he chosen the finest toy-shop in Brighton for cover. He was fast learning the tactics of the chase.

They came with suspenseful slowness, stopping at several other shop-fronts before they reached the toy-shop. It was double-fronted. In the first window a topical set-piece had been mounted, hundreds of toy soldiers engaged in battle. *'The 4th (Royal Irish) Dragoon Guards on the Field of Tel-el-Kebir,'* announced a card. *'We salute our Heroes on their Return to Brighton.'* Jason left his mother and pressed face and hands against the glass.

'It accounts for the flags all over the town,' Guy was saying to her in that insufferably conceited voice, as they came within earshot. 'The 4th have their barracks somewhere out along the Lewes Road, you know. Any excuse for a bit of flag-waving. I suppose we shan't be able to move for the militia after tomorrow. It's really too bad when one has booked for the season.'

She did not answer. She stood behind Jason and submitted to the spell of the toy-shop window, looking past the battle-field, which was lined with soldiers of all Her Majesty's Imperial armies, like unfavoured guests at a ball. The dolls on the shelves at the back had caught her fancy, pretty porcelain things with real hair and perfect clothes in miniature. Moscrop watched her from his position in the shop entrance, through the glass angle of the projecting shop-front. He was near enough to hear every word they said, and they would recognise him at any moment, but he wanted to prolong watching her through the glass until the last possible second.

It was Guy who interrupted his reverie. 'Look who is here,

stepmother. Jason's guardian angel.' Spoken without a trace of good will, nor even the courtesy of touching his cap.

'Mr. Moscrop! But darling, how absolutely charming to meet you again.'

What a gulf there was between these two!

'The pleasure is all mine, Ma'am, I assure you,' said Moscrop. 'I trust that your little boy suffered no aftereffects from his adventure the other day.'

'Good God no. The brat's as tough as a mountain goat. But, my dear, I shudder every time I see that dreadful groyne where you found him. You're a hero, did I tell you? I'm dashed if I know why Brighton gets excited over battles in Egypt when acts of valour are performed by spunky little shopkeepers on its own beach.'

'Thank you, Ma'am.'

'But that's what's so ridiculous, my chuck—we *haven't* thanked you. You wouldn't let me tell Prothero.'

'Quite proper, Ma'am.'

'But there must be *something* I can do.'

'Since you mention it, Ma'am, there is one small matter over which'—he coughed discreetly—'you might indulge me.'

'Of course! What is that?'

'Allow me to renew my acquaintance with young Jason. We were becoming quite firm friends. I should dearly like to take him into this establishment and purchase some small memento for him.'

'Memento? Darling, I couldn't possibly allow that! We are in *your* debt.'

He raised his bowler politely. 'Then with all due respect,

Ma'am, you have no choice but to let me have my way. Come, Jason.'

The child took his hand obediently and they went inside. He hoped to find a wooden telescope, but the plan was frustrated. Almost everything else was available, hoops, tops, toy guns, model yachts, cricket bats. Even, suspended ominously over the counter, a selection of birch-rods. He allowed Jason to make his own choice from the variety of playthings the assistant produced.

The others were waiting when they came out into the sunshine. 'My stars, Jason, how lucky you are!' said his mother. 'What a beautiful thing! What is it, Mr. Moscrop?'

'A wooden crocodile, Ma'am. Once it was placed in his hands he wouldn't let go of it. The jaws open and close like nutcrackers, you see. I don't think he can injure himself with it.'

'He's partial to crocodiles,' said Guy, with a sly smile at Bridget. 'Most civil of you to stand treat to my stepbrother in this way, sir. Now we must be moving on. I was planning on a swim before lunch. Good-day to you.'

'Perhaps Mr. Moscrop is going our way,' said Zena, with emphasis.

'As it happens, I had it in mind to take a look at the sea, Ma'am.'

'Splendid! Then we shall all go together.'

They passed down the street without much conversation, Guy, since it suited him, demonstrating his role as protector and marching moodily between Moscrop and Zena. Bridget followed, with Jason in the push-chair repeatedly snapping the crocodile jaws.

'Guy likes to bathe farther along, towards the West Pier,' said Zena, when they reached the promenade.

'That's the direction I planned to take, Ma'am, if I'm not intruding, that is.'

There was a blustery wind, splendidly invigorating, but difficult for a lady to contend with. She managed her dress and hat with that elegance that was natural to her, but she was unable to walk quickly enough for Guy. 'Let's have my costume and towel, dammit,' he finally called over his shoulder to Bridget. 'I'm going ahead.' As he went, Moscrop took his place beside Zena and the sea shimmered with a brilliance he had not been aware of before.

'None of us is allowed to enjoy the day before Guy has had his swim,' said Zena. 'If his pa knew he was bathing from the beach I don't know what he would do. Prothero says the water is polluted. Cholera and typhus. But hundreds of others are just as much at risk, aren't they? I can't stop the wretched boy from going in, so I don't try.'

'He gives the impression of being a strong-willed young man,' ventured Moscrop.

'He suffers from asthma periodically. We try not to cross him for fear of bringing on an attack. Prothero has made quite a study of the disease. Guy's natural ma was a sufferer, too. Lord, darling, what a breeze this is! Let's sit in the wind-shelter there for five minutes.'

Bridget, in keeping with her status, remained standing beside the push-chair. As soon as it stopped, Jason threw his crocodile on the pavement and made noises of protest.

'Push the little fiend along the promenade for a short way

and come back,' Zena ordered, adding, for Moscrop's ears, 'The girl has no idea how to keep a child amused. Prothero was off his head when he engaged her. She can do no wrong in his eyes. Once he's made up his mind, he's implacable. Guy's the same.'

'That must make life difficult for you.'

'Difficult? My dear, if my lips weren't sealed I'd tell you a tale more harrowing than you'll find in any penny dreadful.'

'A problem in the family, Ma'am?'

'It's made my marriage a continuous ordeal, darling, and I can't disclose a word of it, not even to Jason's gallant rescuer. That child is my one consolation, the undivided joy of my existence. A noisy little pup, I'll grant you, but if I lost *him* it would be the end of everything. You may imagine how I felt the other afternoon.'

'Absolutely. Tell me, is your husband visiting former patients again today?'

There was not a trace of hesitation in her answer. 'Why yes. Prothero's the most generous-hearted man alive, darling, known through the county for his companionable ways. Everyone recognises him when we walk out in Dorking. He has a joke that if someone would invent a machine for raising hats it would be more use to him than his stethoscope. He keeps a book with the names and addresses of all his former patients and he visits them at every opportunity. He's the world's worst at writing letters, so he goes in person and surprises them. He's always sure of a cup of tea and sometimes something more.'

Moscrop blinked, thinking of Lewes Crescent. 'It must

make excessive demands on his time. Not easy for you, I should think, being alone.'

'Not quite alone. I have Jason, my dear. And Guy and Bridget are never far away. You're right, though. I miss Prothero more than he knows. Why am I telling you all this, Mr. Moscrop? You don't want to listen to a woman's nonsense.'

He looked earnestly into the bright eyes. 'Not nonsense at all, Ma'am. I count it a privilege to listen to you. I only wish there were some way in which I could help with the— er—crisis you spoke of.'

'That? Foget about it, darling. An unspeakable thing. Unique to our family. We've faced the worst of it and made our arrangements. We all agreed not to speak of it during these weeks. Shall we walk on now? I've recovered my breath a little.'

He took his place on the side of her nearest the kerb and they did battle again with the breeze as far as the Grand. A riding instructor passed, leading a cavalcade of black-habited, pink-cheeked girls, veils flapping against their hats. Today they held no more interest than the rest of the King's Road traffic. He was far too occupied with what he had just heard. *An unspeakable thing*. What could she mean? A bereavement? Unlikely—the family were not in mourning. What was the other expression she had used? *A tale more harrowing than you'll find in any penny dreadful.* Exaggeration? Even allowing generously for her flamboyant style of rhetoric, it was clear that something markedly unpleasant had happened in the Prothero family. His first thought—that the husband's indiscretions were to blame had to be discounted when she spoke of Prothero with such undisguised affection. Either she suspected nothing, or the most generous-hearted man alive was lucky enough to be married to the most generous-hearted woman.

'This is far enough for me, darling,' she said when they reached Hobden's baths. 'I generally sit on the beach, but it's too gusty today. I shall watch Guy from here.'

He nodded. No lady would take up a position any closer to the gentlemen's bathing station. 'I must take my leave then, Ma'am. It's been a pleasure walking with you. Perhaps I shall see something of you and your family in town tomorrow when the regiment returns. Are you going to watch the homecoming?'

'I'm sure we shall. Jason will adore the uniforms and the brass band. Where's the best position, do you think?'

'I don't know Brighton very well, but I think I shall try to secure a place in the Old Steine—on the Pavilion side. Shall you be attending the civic reception at the Dome tomorrow evening?'

'Sweetheart, I didn't know one had been arranged. I'm not at my best in the evenings, which is a shame, because that's the only time I see Prothero, apart from breakfast.'

'You get tired, I expect. The sea-air is very exhausting.'

'Not really. Almost the reverse, darling. My brain is over-active, Gregory says. He must be right, because I can't sleep without the preparation he gives me. Isn't it convenient being married to a doctor?'

'He gives you a sleeping-draught?'

'Something like that. Oh look! There's Guy going down to the water. I wonder if he'll look round and wave. He likes to be noticed. They do at his age. Have you seen him with his tin of snuff? For all the world like a man of forty.'

'Do you take this potion every night, Ma'am?'

'Without fail, darling, ever since the trouble I mentioned. You see, since then I get into a nervous state about nothing at all. Simply sitting in a room with Prothero and Guy is enough to start my hands shaking. Isn't it ridiculous? There he goes, straight in, without hesitating. That boy loves the water. Oh God! The button's come off my jacket. It's all right. I can sew it on again. Nothing to be concerned about.'

'So you take the potion to alleviate your nervous mani-festations?'

'Exactly, darling. It's miraculous. I lose consciousness in no time at all. Prothero usually suggests I take it imme-diately after dinner. By eight I'm insensible. I swear that sometimes I'm asleep before Jason! You don't think it's dangerous, do you?'

Moscrop looked across the beach, evading the question. 'Your stepson is certainly a strong swimmer. How do you feel when you wake up?'

'Like a print gown after five washings, darling. It takes half-a-dozen sniffs at my *sal volatile* to make me believe I'm alive.'

'What kind of sleeping draught is it?'

Her eyes opened wide, like a child's. 'That's what bothers me, my dear. I don't know. Prothero doesn't tell me, and I don't like to enquire. I believe he prepares it from white crystals that he keeps in a jar, but I've never enquired too closely what they are. I shouldn't want him to think I don't trust him.'

'Perhaps someone else could help.'

'Darling, I'd quite forgotten that you were a medical man. But how charming! It will so relieve my mind.'

What had he volunteered for? 'Medicine isn't quite my field, Ma'am. Optics, you understand.'

'But of course you know about these things! How marvellous of you to go to so much trouble.'

'I dare say that if you could obtain a small sample of the solution I could get it analysed somewhere in the town,' he conceded. 'Though I'm sure your husband can be depended upon.'

'So am I, Mr. Moscrop, so am I. But if your chemist found that the medicine were a trifle strong, perhaps I could prepare a weaker solution without offending Prothero. It's just a little unnerving being insensible for thirteen hours at a time, you understand.'

'Quite so, Ma'am. When would you be able to obtain this sample for me? It would have to be done unobtrusively, would it not?'

'Darling, you're so perspicacious! If you came to the croquet lawn at the Albemarle at two this afternoon, I could leave Bridget dressing Jason. Prothero will be in the billiards-room with Guy. How droll—we shall feel like two conspirators!'

8

THE HEROES OF TEL-EL-KEBIR marched down the Grand
Parade in ranks of eight to the tune of *Slap Bang, Here We
Are Again* and all Brighton lined the pavements to welcome
them. The war in Egypt had been a daily topic of conversation
for months past, quite as compelling as the scares about the
town's drainage system. The local newspapers carried long
dispatches from Cairo, and in the aquarium entrance hall a
huge canvas map of the seat of war was mounted among the
weighing-machines, with flags to indicate the latest positions of the English and Egyptian armies. When the return
of the Royal Irish was announced, a full civic reception was
arranged at once, but the spontaneous tribute of almost the
entire population quite stole the Corporation's thunder.
Flags appeared everywhere, even draped over the lichen on
the walls of the poorest houses. Humble cab-horses trotted
through the town with trimmings of red, white and blue;

children appeared in miniature tropical helmets, brandish-
ing tin swords; the minstrel bands played little else but *See
the Conquering Hero Comes* and *When Johnny Comes Marching
Home.*

As soon as Moscrop reached the Old Steine he saw that
there was small chance of picking out the Protheros, even
if Zena had managed to persuade her husband that this was
the best vantage-point. It was like The Mall on Coronation
Day. Crowds nine or ten deep lined the route from the
Pavilion to St. Peter's. Latecomers were improvising peri-
scopes with hand mirrors, or resorting to the trees. The
police, massively reinforced, had linked arms to preserve a
passage for the regiment.

'Was you wishing you had your spy-glass?'

He turned in surprise, stung by the pertinence of the
question. It was *exactly* what he had been wishing. Bridget
stood there, smiling mysteriously. 'You wouldn't spot the
doctor and his wife in this mob, sir. Neither of 'em's over-
tall, and they started out late, long after the crowds began
to collect.'

'You! How strange! I had no idea—'

'Not so strange as you think, sir.' She tilted her hat so
that two of its imitation cherries lolled coquettishly over the
brim. 'I've been following you for ten minutes or more.'

'*Following* me?' Whatever was the girl saying?

'You ain't the only one that plays follow my leader.
I waited for you at the top of North Street, near the
Penitents' Home. I knew you'd come that way because your
diggings are in Montpelier Parade. That's given you food
for thought, hasn't it?'

'I don't understand.' For the first time he looked at Bridget without regard to status. Her manner verged on impertinence and he would certainly have silenced the girl if she had not caught him unprepared. In the most presumptuous way she was demanding a conversation on equal terms. There was a positive hint of archness in the set of her mouth, as if she had caught him prowling below stairs. A neat little face, too, for all its pertness. Until now he had not noticed. 'What possible reason do you have for following me?'

She stepped closer and, as if it were the most natural thing to do, tucked her hand behind his right arm. 'If you was to buy me a glass of white satin you might find out.'

He stiffened. Into a public house to drink gin with a domestic? The very idea!

He treated the suggestion with contemptuous silence. But he did not remove the offending hand from his arm.

'You won't see much of the military from here,' she persisted. 'Just the tops of their hats. We could have a much more profitable half-hour together. The Seven Stars is just around the corner.'

And this was to have been the year when he made his debut in the Brighton season!

'There won't be a soul in the bar. They've all come on the streets for the march-past. Don't let's lose time. You want to find out some more about Mrs. P., don't you?'

Put like that, it sounded appallingly crude, but he had to admit that the girl had the native gift of shrewdness one sometimes found among females of the lower orders. She was right. If there was anything to be learned of Zena, then he was enslaved. Feeling much as he had when he abandoned Bernhardt for his night at the Canterbury, he permitted Bridget to guide him towards Ship Street by way of Bartholomews. The salute was going to be taken from the Town Hall steps, so the pavement opposite bristled with people determined not to budge from hard-won positions. She steered him determinedly through the crush, at times surprising him with pressures he could not recall having experienced among the crowds in Oxford Street or at Waterloo Station.

A pink awning had been erected in front of the Town Hall, and the civic dignitaries and some of the senior officers of the regiment and their ladies were ranged under it in tiers. They made a brave show, a suitable focus of attention, medallions, civic regalia, ermine, gold braid, bright red Eton jackets. But the limelight was stolen by the milliners; you could hardly see a face for the hats, and you could hardly see the hats for the trimmings, ostrich feathers, swansdown, fruit, flowers and humming birds.

'Gorgeous, don't you think?' demanded Bridget, cherries bobbing aggressively.

'Unparalleled.'

'*She's* there, of course.'

'She is? Where?'

'In the second row, third from the right, wearing white lilac and convulvulus. They're artificial.'

He stared between shifting parasols, expecting to be rewarded with a glimpse of Zena's haunting features. 'The second row, you say. I don't see her. That isn't your mistress, Bridget. She doesn't have copper hair. Good Lord!'

'Not *my* mistress,' said Bridget, with emphasis. They were looking at the young woman from Lewes Crescent, Dr. Prothero's riding-companion.

'What is she doing up there?'

'Don't you know who she is? That's Miss Samantha Floyd-Whittingham, the daughter of the Colonel. She's very well known in Brighton. Her father has set her up in a big house on the front. They say it's because he won't trust her in the officer's quarters with so many men about. Instead she has the run of Brighton, and the Colonel thinks she sits indoors counting seagulls from her window.'

Five minutes later they were seated in an almost deserted tap-room.

'You know who that was, don't you?' said Bridget.

'Miss Floyd-Whittingham, you mean? A friend of Dr. Prothero's I believe.'

'Friend! You've got a fine sense of humour, sir.'

They sipped at their drinks, watching each other.

'How did the doctor meet this young woman?' asked Moscrop.

'I couldn't tell you. He's a ladies' man, as you must have seen for yourself. It's obvious to everyone but his wife. I've had to remind him of his position once or twice myself, I might say. I think it must have been last year he was intro-duced to her, at one of them musical evenings. We come to Brighton each year, you know. He's always been one for going out and about, and the mistress thinks nothing of it. She believes everything he tells her. Has she told you about the patients he's supposed to be visiting every afternoon? Patients! I ask you!'

'Such an unlikely woman to be deceived,' observed Moscrop, almost to himself. 'Who would credit it? One has only to hear her speak—that sparkling conversation. An emancipated woman in every syllable she utters.'

Bridget smirked. 'That shows how much you know about the fair sex. It ain't the quiet ones that lose their husbands, Mr. Moscrop, it's Mrs. Prothero and her kind, bubbling over so passionate they don't notice their men creeping out the back door. Or won't admit to it.'

'You know what is going on between the doctor and this person, then?'

'Everyone does—except my mistress. I don't think she'd see it if they was sitting on her own sofa holding hands, poor woman. You've taken a fancy to her, haven't you?'

'Never mind,' said Moscrop. There were limits to plain speaking.

Bridget was not so easily deflected. 'I've seen you with the glasses to your eyes, Mr. Moscrop, and I've watched you on the beach and outside the hotel when the mistress hasn't known you were there. I take you for a man that goes to a great deal of trouble to get what he wants. I saw you talking to the bathing-machine woman the other day when I was in the water with Guy. Oh, don't concern yourself. It don't bother me what you've seen or what she told you. I wouldn't be the first of my sort to give a little tuition to the gentry—not that Guy needs much. Takes after his father, I can tell you, and that's why I've no fears from that quarter. But you're different, aren't you? You wouldn't make a pass at me if I invited you. Single-minded, that's you.'

Was this meant for provocation, or was the girl trying

to make a point? Either way, the conversation had taken a personal turn he was determined to correct.

'If you know that Mrs. Prothero is being deceived by her husband, why don't you tell her?'

'I've got my *character* to consider,' said Bridget, her voice pitched high in protest. 'I can't afford to cross the doctor. I'd never obtain another position if he gave me a bad character. That's what I was coming to, anyway. What's to be gained if she does find out about him? Nothing. It'll send her mad or break her heart. She's so blind to his doings that he don't even bother to brush the red hairs off his jacket collar.'

'But if her husband is unfaithful—'

'You think the knowledge of it might throw her into another's arms? Don't believe it, sir. Oh, I know you've watched her by the hour. You're a patient man, I don't deny it, and you deserve something for your persistence. I've followed each stage of it, the binocular-work, the day you brought back Jason, the meeting at the toy-shop and yesterday I watched from the window as she took some of her sleeping-draught to you at the croquet-lawn. Do you expect to find there's arsenic in it, Mr. Moscrop? Do you think he's killing her? Of course he ain't! He's perfectly content with things the way they are.'

'I had no such thought. I was simply doing a lady a good turn.' Really, Bridget was altogether too uppish. A chit of a servant-wench addressing him like this! He should have walked out at once. If the subject of their conversation were not so riveting he would certainly have done so.

'Take my word for it,' she continued. 'She's the same with everyone—generous, warm-hearted and open in her speech. It don't mean a thing, Mr. Moscrop. There's only one man for her and that's my master, with all his faults. If you tell her about them she won't thank you for it. Take as many walks as you like with her, try all your charms on her—who am I to say you haven't no chance at all? But one thing I do ask of you—and this is why I had to find you this morning—don't tell her the truth about her husband, sir. God knows what will happen if you do.'

■ He was glad he chose to walk along the front that evening in preference to the route through the town. The sound of the waves on the shingle was infinitely clearer by night. It synchronised with some small pulse in his brain, calming his mood and stabilizing his thoughts, like the tick of the grandfather clock downstairs when he was alone at night as a child. He could begin to feel in control again. He was so unused to being involved in people's lives, least of all in the secrets of man and wife. Oh, he had seen infidelities enough through his glasses—anyone with sharp observation and a good memory for faces could pick out three or four in a fortnight by the sea—but he had always remained quite detached from the parties involved. In the present case he had deliberately eschewed the glasses, and—he admitted it—surrendered his objectivity. Complications were inevitable in the circumstances. Now it was necessary to resolve them in as calm and business-like a manner as possible. He had started this and he would see it through.

Ahead, a shaft of moonlight bisected the sea, to form a continuous line with the lantern-reflections under the

Chain Pier. The chill of autumn had kept all but a handful of stalwarts off the front. Most were soldiers in town on a pass, a girl on one arm, swagger-stick under the other, pork-pie hat rakishly askew, spurs jingling long after they passed.

Near the aquarium he fancied he could hear voices coming from the beach. The glow of gas-lamps on the promenade made it difficult to see much below, and in the usual way he would not have tried to distinguish who was down there. By all accounts the nocturnal activities on the pebbles were not intended to be overseen. Nor did they usually involve much conversation. But he was sure, as he came nearer, that several men were down there tonight, engaging in animated talk. And hammering. There were no boats so far along for them to be working on. He drew level with the clock-tower and approached the promenade-railing, shading his eyes with both hands.

There must have been a dozen men in a working-party sinking stakes into the shingle near the water's edge. Farther along, he made out a line of uprights jutting starkly against the glinting luminosity of the water. Some were twice as tall as the men and had cross-pieces fixed with diagonal struts. If this had not been Brighton—and in the season—he would have sworn that he was looking at a row of gibbets. He shivered, pulled up his overcoat collar and moved away towards the Marine Parade at a tidy step, without accounting for what he had seen.

The Albemarle was situated in a favoured position overlooking the Chain Pier, its crenellated facade and porticoed entrance proclaiming it one of the more exclusive hotels in a fashionable terrace. The crimson velvet curtains at the dining-room windows were only half-drawn, so that passers-by were treated to glimpses of waiters dancing attendance with silver coffee-pots. Moscrop paced the pavement oppo-site, like a sentry. Cabs were beginning to line the kerbs in anticipation of trade; this evening most would be making for the Dome. The ball in the regiment's honour was certain to be one of the principal events of the season.

He took out his watch and held it to the light. Half past eight, she had said, and it was already twenty minutes to nine. Perhaps it was less easy to slip away unobtrusively than she had thought.

The hotel door opened and a figure emerged. Not Zena, unhappily. A man in full evening dress, with cape and stick. As he stepped forward to secure a cab, his face passed close to the ornamental lamp attached to one of the columns. Dr. Prothero, for sure. The spry movements would have given him away if the lamp had not. He was across the pavement and into a growler so fast that he might have been going to a patient in labour. The driver executed a neat turn in the road and made off in the direction of Black Rock and—Moscrop reflected—Lewes Crescent.

Others followed at intervals, couples mostly, fussing over their gowns and cloaks as they negotiated the carriage-steps. Almost nine o'clock. Had she forgotten? With Prothero gone, what could be keeping her?

On turning, he practically collided with a female figure wrapped in a shawl.

'What the devil . . . ?' She had appeared from nowhere.

'Hello, Mr. Moscrop.'

Bridget's voice, dammit. She drew back the shawl a little and he could see that malapert little face beaming delightedly at the effect it produced on him.

'Caught you by surprise, didn't I? There's another entrance round the corner and scarcely anyone uses it. Have you got the formula for my mistress?'

'I was intending to hand it to her personally.'

'Well you can't, can you? She ain't here. Oh, yes, I've to tell you that she's sorry she can't come down. She took to her bed straight after dinner to please Dr. Prothero—him being set on an evening out and wanting to see her asleep before he went.'

'Asleep, you say. Did she take the sleeping-draught?'

Bridget winked in a most embarrassing fashion. 'No, she was foxing when he looked in on her. She's taking no more of that stuff until she hears from you. But of course she can't come down here in her night-things, and nor could you go up, being a gentleman.'

'Indeed not!'

'So that's why I've been sent down, to act as messenger. Have you found out what it is she's been taking?'

He felt in his breast pocket for the piece of blue paper on which the chemist had summarised the result of his analysis. 'Perhaps you will kindly convey this to Mrs. Prothero, then. It will set her mind at rest. The preparation is nothing more sinister than chloral hydrate. You probably know it as chloral. Thousands dose themselves with it to induce sleep. Taken to excess, it can produce a morbid condition known as chloralism, but the solution your mistress has is unlikely to have that effect.'

'I told you he wasn't poisoning her.'

'There has never been any suggestion that he was. I think you should guard your tongue, young lady. Good God! What was that?'

A crack like a pistol-shot from behind them. Someone along the street screamed in fright. A dog started barking. Faces appeared at the hotel windows.

'It came from down on the beach, I'm certain,' said Bridget.

They went to the railing and leaned over. People ran across the road from the hotels and joined them.

'Some half-drunk soldier showing off to his doxy,' someone decided.

'They don't carry arms when they're off duty.'

'Could have filched a rifle from the shooting-gallery.'

'Look!' said Bridget. 'There's people down there. With flares. D'you think they've found a corpse?'

Moscrop remembered the strange constructions he had seen. The activity appeared to be taking place at about the same spot. They moved with the crowd to get a closer view. They had not gone more than a few yards when there was another sensation down below. A spluttering of flame, a violent hissing sound, and the sight of a luminous projectile speeding skywards and dipping into a spectacular parabola over the sea.

'A blooming sky-rocket! It's a firework show in honour of the military.'

It was, and the function of the gibbet-like structures was made clear. They were for the mounting of the set-pieces, the climax of all pyrotechnic displays. Splendid initiative on someone's part! One hoped that the tableaux would include some fitting tribute to the regiment. Already the town was answering the summons of that first rocket, coming on to the streets in scores and converging on the sea-front. Young men clambered over the railing from the Marine Parade on to the roof of the Aquarium for a grandstand view. Children still flushed with the warmth of sleep were brought into the night air wrapped in blankets, their eyes registering half-excitement, half-apprehension.

'I'm dotty about fireworks,' said Bridget. 'Sky-rockets. Oh, lovely!'

'Shouldn't you return to your mistress? She must wonder what is happening.'

'You're right. I'll have a better view from up there. Her room and Jason's overlook the beach. We're on the second floor—those windows on the right. Look, there's Guy on the balcony! Wave your umbrella.'

'He wouldn't see us, among so many,' said Moscrop drily. 'You won't forget to give the formula to Mrs. Prothero, will you? Do you think if I waited here I might see her come out on to the balcony? I suppose not. She will not want to put all her clothes back on for a few skyrockets. She can probably see all she wants from the other side of the window. Then she can take her chloral in total confidence and be sleeping when her husband returns. You will remember me to her, won't you?'

The girl made a curious sound in her throat which began as a gurgle and ended as a gale of immodest laughter. 'She won't need no remembering of you, Mr. Moscrop. You ain't the sort of man she's likely to forget!'

Deuced impertinence! What the girl meant by her remark he was not sure, but he was damned certain he was not going to allow a domestic to treat him with open derision. He took a breath to deliver a crushing rejoinder, but there was no one to crush. She had turned away, still laughing, and made her escape through the crowd.

A row of Catherine Wheels made a spluttering start on the beach. He turned to look at the Albemarle again. The balcony was empty. It was impossible to see whether anyone was within. The crowd was thick around him, but for once he did not experience any pleasure in being shoulder to shoulder with a mass of people he did not know. Nor did fireworks interest him. There were better shows every Saturday at the Crystal Palace. In ten minutes, he took a last look at the hotel window and edged through the crowd, to begin the walk back along the front to his lodgings.

On the beach, a crocodile made its appearance, the first of the set-pieces, symbolic of Egypt, its jaw opening and closing wickedly. What cheers there were as the sparks spent themselves and the enemy was exposed as a charred and smoking ruin! Marvellous to be British, and in Brighton, and secure from such monsters!

CHAPTER

9

'IT'S A CURIOUS THING, Sarge,' Constable Thackeray observed.

'What is?'

'Why, that anyone should think of putting an end to one of his fellow beings at the seaside. A most peculiar thing. I've always thought of a holiday as a pleasurable experience. Not that I know a lot about it. The only days I've had by the sea have been the "M" Division excursions to Southend, and I don't usually have much recollection of them. But it stands to reason, Sarge. Murder's got nothing to do with donkey-rides and sand-castles and—er—'

'Punch and Judy?' suggested Sergeant Cribb. 'You're talking through your hat, Thackeray. Murder's got *every-thing* to do with the seaside. All that's curious is that there isn't more of it.' The argument demolished, he returned to his *Brighton and Sussex Daily Post*, thoughtfully purchased at London Bridge. The two detectives were seated in a second-class carriage of the Brighton Express. Five tunnels and numerous long stretches of chalk embankment tended to keep observation of the countryside to a minimum. Cribb, fox-faced and short of small-talk, had his newspaper. Thackeray, rhino-hided and implacable, was bent on conversation.

'The whole atmosphere's against it, Sarge. Sunshine. Promenading. Concert parties.' Seeing that Cribb was not preparing to respond, he extended the list indefinitely. 'A plate of winkles. Trips on the *Skylark*. Minstrel shows. A sniff of the briny from the pier-head . . .'

Cribb put down his newspaper. 'When we get to Brighton, Constable, there won't be much time for sight-seeing, but I want you to make sure you get a look at that pier you're talking about. There's two of 'em where we're going, paper-doily things, with fancy iron-work all white and smelling of fresh paint. When you've had your eyeful of the scrubbed decks and the dapper little buildings, take a look underneath, right under the pier. I'll tell you what you'll see. Girders festering with barnacles. Slime and weed and water black as pitch lurching and heaving round the under-structure fit to turn your stomach. That's part of your pier, too. Just as slums and alleys and back-streets lie behind the nobby hotels along the sea-front. Some can close their eyes to 'em. Not you and me, Thackeray. We ain't going to Brighton for a paddle, you know.'

Thackeray calmly stroked the underside of his beard with the back of his hand and studied the cocoa-advertisement a foot above Cribb's bowler hat. He was too experienced to be baited by sarcasm of that sort. Cribb, denied satisfaction, found it impossible to return to his reading.

'Nothing to do with the seaside? That's one of the best I've heard—even from you. If you'd only widen your reading, Constable, you'd know there's hardly a street in Brighton without its murderous associations.' He began counting off the fingers on his left hand. 'The King's Road. Charles Bravo met his wife there. Portland Street, where Christiana Edmunds took her poisoned chocolates to be sold. Queen's Square, where Constance Kent confessed to murdering her stepbrother. Lover's Walk, Preston, where John William Holloway wheeled the pieces of his wife on a barrow and buried 'em. He was a painter on the Chain Pier, smartening it up for the likes of you to sniff the briny from. I could go on.'

'Don't, Sarge. I shall never enjoy another "M" Division outing. What makes 'em choose the seaside, do you think?'

'Obvious reasons. Place is full of strangers right through the summer. Irregular behaviour isn't noticed. People tend to be more conversational on holiday, too. Chance of making casual acquaintances.'

'You're right, now I come to think about it. You couldn't find a better place for a spot of murdering.'

'Accidental deaths are happening all the time,' said Cribb, warming to his theme. 'There's one reported in the paper here. Woman of fifty-five found drowned. Non-swimmer. Seems she took a dip on the last day of her holiday. Ashamed to take a dry costume back to London, so she went for an early morning bathe, when not many people were about. Now who's to know whether someone didn't hold her head under?'

'Blimey, Sarge, you've got a suspicious mind.'

'I don't say it happened, but it could have. And if she wasn't murdered, what about the cove that falls off the pier next week, or the one that swims out too far the week after? It's Lombard Street to a china orange that sooner or later some evil-minded person will see it as a neat way of dispatching a victim.'

'Well, *you* have, Sarge.'

'Exactly. You've got to learn to think as they do, Constable. We wouldn't be much help to the Brighton force if we couldn't. They're looking to you and me for something special in the way of detective-work. It's not like them to call in the Yard unless they're driven to it. Put the winkles out of your mind, Thackeray, and use the rest of the journey to set your thoughts in order for a piece of smart investigating.'

Two tunnels on, Thackeray caught Cribb's eye again, in transit from *Social Intelligence* to *In the Magistrates' Court*. 'Sarge, why did you make that remark about Punch and Judy? I can't see what connection it has with murder. It's children's entertainment after all.'

Cribb was silent, disinclined to relate the criminal career of Mr. Punch for the benefit of his assistant.

'Part of any seaside holiday,' Thackeray persisted.

Cribb spoke without looking up. 'Constable, there was one other murder I should have mentioned earlier. A year ago, on this very line, a Mr. Gold was done to death in the Brighton Express by one Lefroy, whose effigy is now in Madame Tussaud's. If you ask me one more question I guarantee there'll soon be a likeness of me standing beside him in the waxworks. Just think *that* out and let me read my newspaper.'

■ Grafton Street, where they had been asked to report, proved to be a turning off the Marine Parade, as handsome a setting for a police station as either detective had encountered. Constabulary duties in such surroundings could not be anything but delightful. The cab-drive along the front, besides introducing them to the champagne quality of the sea air, afforded glimpses of a way of life seldom seen anywhere in London but Hyde Park. Society beauties paraded in open carriages, warding off the undesirable effects of the sun with lace parasols, and contriving simultaneously to be seen to advantage from both sides of the road. Others rode on horseback or walked beside young men in blazers and straw hats. In the background the waves lazily unfurled and sent dazzling white foam racing up the shingle. What a beat for some fortunate bobby to pound!

The atmosphere inside the station was just as balmy. 'A pot of fresh tea, if you please, Constable Murphy,' called the duty sergeant as they entered. 'It's either two gentlemen what've come to confess to stealing a pair of boots each, size twelve, or the reinforcements from the Yard are here. Good afternoon, gentlemen. Privileged to meet you. Brown's my name and Pink's my Inspector's. Singular, don't you think? I'd better take you straight in to him. Murphy will take care of your things.' Inspector Pink was misnamed. His face bore witness to thirty summers or more of service on the south coast, as brown and creased as one of last season's potatoes. 'Uncommon glad to see you, gentlemen. It's not often that we get a case that we know straight away is quite beyond the skills of our own detectives. Extraordinary affair, this. He damned near got away with it, too. If it hadn't been for a sharp-eyed young lad, he certainly would have.'

'There was a witness to the crime, then?' said Cribb.

'No, more's the pity. Don't know where it happened, or when. This boy was smart enough to spot the evidence, that's all. He reported it to the manager, who came straight to us this morning. It's still in place. We couldn't have moved it if we'd wanted. You'll see why. If you're not too tired, we'll go along as soon as you finish your tea. It's just a short walk from here.'

The inspector was clearly determined not to spoil the impact of his evidence *in situ* by saying any more about it, so with respect for his feelings they stirred and sipped and blew on their tea to such effect that they were marching along the Marine Parade in minutes, leaving Sergeant Brown to marvel over the prodigious capacities of the Scotland Yard palate.

■ 'I'm sure you must have heard of our aquarium,' said the Inspector as he led them down the granite steps. 'Designed by Birch, the fellow who built the West Pier. It's always been a favourite place of mine. There's something about the atmosphere. This is a deuced unfortunate thing to happen. I only hope it won't discourage visitors.'

'The reverse, I should think,' said Cribb.

They strode importantly through the reading-room and along the main aisle, their substantial tread diverting attention from the tanks. Halfway along, a large, uniformed constable was reinforcing a notice announcing that owing to unforeseen circumstances the Alligator and Crocodile

Cavern was temporarily closed. A small man in pince-nez hovered anxiously nearby.

'This is the manager, Mr. Pym,' the Inspector explained. 'Sergeant Cribb and his assistant are from the Criminal Investigation Department, Mr. Pym. They will be conducting this inquiry.'

Mr. Pym advanced a nervous hand. 'Most gratified. I hope that we shall not need to involve the newspapers. It could have such a discouraging effect on attendances.'

'Have you done as I asked?' enquired Inspector Pink.

'Yes. The big one is well-drugged, and I think the others are asleep too. Shall we go inside?'

'We shall need more light,' said the inspector. 'Where did you put the bull's-eyes, Constable?'

'Just inside the door, sir, on your left.'

Even with lanterns lit and probing the interior, the shape and size of the cavern were disconcertingly difficult to make out. 'Your eyes will get accustomed shortly,' Mr. Pym assured them. 'It's perfectly safe to step forward. The specimens are all on the other side of the glass.'

'This is the tank,' said the inspector. '*Crocodylus Niloticus.* D'you see them gentlemen? The ugliest beasts alive. Now, bring your lantern nearer, Sergeant, will you? It won't disturb the crocs. That one with its jaws agape will stay like that for hours.'

'In their natural state they let the tick-birds clear their teeth of leeches,' volunteered Mr. Pym.

'Now take a look at this,' said the inspector. 'Wedged down between the rock and the glass. What do you think of that, gentlemen?'

The lantern beams converged on a section at the base of the tank normally in shadow, the arrangement of the rocks ensuring that the reptiles were kept a yard or so away from the glass. There, in a crevice formed between rock and glass, was a human hand, severed above the wrist and resting on its stump, palm facing outwards.

'The devil of it is,' said Inspector Pink, 'that this is all we've got to go on. Where the rest of the body is you may well conjecture, gentlemen.'

The wicked yellow eyes of the largest inmate of the tank continued to glitter unwinkingly in the artificial light.

'He must have been a sharp lad to spot it down here,' said Cribb. 'Could have lain here a long time. What time was it he saw you, Mr. Pym?'

'Half past nine, I should think. I closed the cavern to visitors and went straight to the police station.'

'And I decided to send a cable to the Yard at once,' added the inspector. 'It was too much for my chaps to tackle—or not enough, rather. What do you propose, Sergeant?'

'I shall need to get the evidence out, take a closer look at it.'

'I thought of that,' the inspector said proudly. 'Mr. Pym has drugged the crocodiles.'

'Fish soaked in morphia,' explained Mr. Pym.

'Have they all eaten some?'

'The big fellow has,' said Mr. Pym, 'and he's the one that matters. The others are docile enough. I'll get a keeper to retrieve the hand at once.'

'No you won't,' said Cribb. 'That's all the evidence I've got. I'm not having it snatched out like a piece of rejected meat. It's got to be handled delicate—by a professional. Thackeray . . .'

'Sergeant?'

'Have you got your gloves with you?'

'Yes, Sarge.'

'Good. All you'll want is a large brown envelope and a lamp to see you don't put your foot on anything. Here's a bull's-eye for you. Can you supply the stationery, Mr. Pym?'

'Why yes, but do you think—'

'Think? Thackeray's a man of action, trained to do his thinking afterwards. You're game, Constable, ain't you?' He's coped with worse than this in his time, gentlemen. Round the back you go with Mr. Pym, Thackeray. You don't have to climb in from here, you know. Careful how you handle the evidence, mind.'

It was probably a distortion caused by the uneven lighting, but momentarily Thackeray appeared to regard his superior with the same disaffected stare that was present in the eyes of the creatures he was about to join. Then he followed Mr. Pym through a door which he unlocked beside the entrance.

Presently there was the sound of unbolting at the rear of the tank.

'Hold it, Thackeray!' called Cribb. 'One of 'em's on the move. Give him a moment to settle down.'

It was a long minute before the lanterns discerned a larger than average foot being lowered from a hinged flap on to the moss-covered rock. Thackeray's stooping figure followed, envelope in one hand, lantern in the other.

'There's nothing in your way,' Cribb quietly advised him,

'but I shouldn't be too long about it. Drugs can wear off, you know.'

A small crocodile, probably frightened, lowered itself into the water to the left with a splash and Thackeray completed the journey to the rocks at the front in two quick strides.

'Splendid,' said Cribb. 'The big one ain't moved a muscle yet. Now hook the hand up careful, man. Put your lantern down a moment, and get your envelope ready or you'll be all fingers and thumbs, if you'll forgive the expression in the circumstances. Careful, now. Ah! Neatly done! There's Scotland Yard training for you, gentlemen. Back you go then, Thackeray. Remember the lantern and don't get cocky now. The tails can be just as vicious as the teeth.'

At the Grafton Street police station they took a closer look at the evidence, which Thackeray had carried along the Marine Parade in its brown envelope like an excursionist clutching his packet of sandwiches. Cribb spread several sheets of white paper across Inspector Pink's desk and they took the severed member out and placed it palm downwards for examination.

'What's your opinion, Thackeray?'

'Blimey, Sarge, the cases don't get no easier, do they? We've had our troubles trying to identify headless corpses, but I think this is the least we've ever had to go on.' He leaned over it speculatively. 'It's a woman's or a boy's, I reckon. Too narrow for a man's. And the nails look as though they was polished.'

'Good. Anything else?'

There was a pause as Thackeray secretly studied the arrangement of his own fingers and thumbs. 'It's a right hand, Sarge.'

'I'm bound to agree. Pity it wasn't the left, or we might have found the mark of a wedding ring. What about the state of the fingers?'

Thackeray turned the hand over. 'Well, there's no blisters or hard skin here. I don't think it's done a lot of manual work. This don't look like the hand of a seamstress or a factory girl. It could belong to a lady.'

'Possibly,' said Cribb. 'What are your feelings on the matter, sir?'

Inspector Pink cleared his throat. 'Lady? Yes, a lady. That's good thinking, Constable. A lady. Yes, I'm bound to agree with you there. I think you've summed it up.'

'You don't think the hand can tell us anything else?' said Cribb.

'Ah! That's another matter. I didn't say that, did I? Oh no, not at all.'

'What did you have in mind then, sir?'

'In mind?' Inspector Pink frowned. 'You tell me what's in your mind first, Sergeant. I wouldn't want to steal the thunder of a Scotland Yard man.'

'Well, sir, let's take a look at the point where the wrist was severed.'

Thackeray and the inspector approached as closely as they felt able to.

'Devilish powerful jaws these crocodiles have,' the inspector remarked.

'Now that's just the point, sir,' said Cribb. 'I don't believe this was done by a crocodile. It's far too neat for that. I'm no authority on the species, but I'd expect a crocodile's teeth to leave their shape on something they cut through, not a surface as clean as this. There ought to be some fluting in the cut, don't you see—rather like the mark your teeth would leave on a crisp apple. I think the job was done with a sharp blade, a cleaver or something similar.'

'By Jove, but that means—'

'You're right, sir—that the hand was cut from the body somewhere else and brought here to be thrown to the reptiles. And if you'll give me ten minutes, your paper-knife and a good magnifying glass, I may be able to tell you where the cutting was done.'

In seconds the room took on the appearance of an operating theatre, with Thackeray in charge of the instruments—to which Cribb added a pair of tweezers from his pocket and a clean handkerchief—and Inspector Pink in attendance as a somewhat apprehensive onlooker.

'I'll need more light,' Cribb said. 'The table-lamp, if you please, Inspector. Spread the handkerchief here, Thackeray. Now, gentlemen, I propose scraping the undersides of the finger-nails. The paper-knife, please.'

After several minutes' careful work a small deposit lay on the white linen.

'Magnifying-glass. Thank you. Would you care to see for yourselves?'

'Sand, by George!' said the inspector. 'She must have been on the beach.'

'Probably,' said Cribb. 'But that ain't much help, is it? Half the people in Brighton must have sand in their finger-nails.'

'Ah!' said the inspector, in a significant tone. 'Not your pure-bred ladies, though. They never go nearer the sea than the pier and the esplanade. The sand disposes of your theory that the hand belonged to a lady, Constable Thackeray.'

'Not necessarily,' said Cribb, working at the point of severance with tweezers and magnifying glass. 'There's sand here too, adhering to the blood. I think the dismembering was done on the beach. The body—if we assume there was one—could have been dragged down there. Now look at these.' He placed four or five tiny opalescent spheres on the handkerchief.

'Fish scales, by Jupiter!'

'I think so, sir. Now, am I right in assuming that the food given to the crocodiles—which included fish, I believe—is passed to them through the hatch at the *rear* of the tank?'

'I'm sure of it.'

'So it is most unlikely that these scales were picked up in the tank, remembering that the hand was at the front, in a place inaccessible to the crocodiles.'

'Indeed, yes.'

'There is a fish market somewhere along the beach, I seem to remember.'

'That is so. Not ten minutes away from here.'

'Capital! Thackeray and I will take another walk, then. I'm curious to see what implements they use for cutting the fish.'

CHAPTER 10

ON THE BEACH NEXT afternoon Albert Moscrop lifted the
newspaper that was serving to screen his face from the sun,
propped himself on one elbow and read the leading article
for the fourth time that day.

A Gruesome Discovery on Brighton Beach

The evidence of a sinister and probably murderous crime
was uncovered yesterday by a team of police officers and
Corporation workmen digging on one of the most frequented sections of the Brighton foreshore, the site of
the fish market. The excavation, which was observed by
a large crowd of holidaymakers and residents, proceeded
under the direction of Sergeant Cribb, a detective of the
Criminal Investigation Department of Scotland Yard, who
was summoned to the town in the morning, consequent
upon the discovery of A SEVERED HUMAN HAND in the

new Alligator and Crocodile Cavern of the Aquarium. This horrifying discovery was made by a schoolboy shortly after the Aquarium opened yesterday morning. The lad, who is understood to be a visitor, drew the attention of the manager, Mr. Pym, to the tank in question. The police were informed without delay, and a decision was made at once to telegraph for the assistance of Scotland Yard.

Sergeant Cribb, an officer who is understood to have investigated successfully a number of murders in the Metropolis in recent years, arrived at Brighton on the 2.15 p.m. train, accompanied by an assistant, and proceeded at once to the police station in Grafton Street, and shortly after to the Aquarium, where the gruesome object of his investigation was extracted from its resting place among the saurians and removed to the police station. The experts from Scotland Yard there conducted a minute examination of the hand, as a consequence of which Sergeant Cribb became convinced that particles of sand and fish scales adhering to it indicated a connection with the fishmarket, some quarter of a mile to the west of the Chain Pier. Orders were issued for AN EXHAUSTIVE SEARCH FOR A SHARP-BLADED INSTRUMENT among the stalls and barrows which comprise the market. A large body of local police was assigned to this task and within a short time Sergeant Cribb was observed to be standing beside a table bearing a formidable haul of knives, cleavers and hand-saws, while the fish-mongering contingent vainly solicited prospective customers to purchase unfilleted sole and plaice.

A suitable weapon not having been identified, the search was extended to the arches under the adjacent promenade, in which nets, pots and other impedimenta of the fishing community are stored. Those tenants of the arches who were present unlocked their premises, but a number of doors had to be forced open on the Sergeant's orders. After some twenty minutes the search was concentrated on a particular arch in which the lock was found to be faulty. Inside, the officers found CLEAR EVIDENCE OF RECENT BLOOD-STAINS on the floor and on several packing cases which appeared to have been utilised as a dissecting table. Nothing else having been found, Sergeant Cribb took the unusual steps of ordering the stretch of beach where the market is situated to be cleared and roped off. Shovels were called for, and reinforcements from the Corporation Works Department were summoned to join the police in the macabre exercise of digging the shingle for human remains.

The activity attracted considerable interest, and before long additional police were called for to patrol the margins of the roped-off area, which were lined with inquisitive spectators, including many YOUNG CHILDREN AND MEMBERS OF THE FAIR SEX. The section of the promenade overlooking the scene was at times impassable, so thick was the concourse, and itinerant vendors of refreshments did a brisk trade.

A selection of objects was uncovered in the first halfhour, providing flurries of excitement among the onlookers, but nothing to interest Sergeant Cribb, the finds consisting in the main of such flotsam and jetsam as may be deposited on any beach, together with the detritus of previous Bank Holiday invasions, stone beer bottles, cutlery mislaid from picnic hampers, and children's beach-implements.

It was towards four o'clock, when interest in the excavation was beginning to flag in favour of thoughts of tea, that one of the workmen uncovered a parcel roughly wrapped in newspaper and buried some eighteen inches below the surface. On being unwrapped, it was found to contain PART OF A HUMAN LEG SEVERED BELOW THE KNEE.

The grisly prize was borne in triumph to Sergeant Cribb, who demonstrated a proper concern for the sensibilities of his audience by immediately ordering the place where it was found to be screened from public view with sheets of canvas improvised from nearby bathing-tents. Digging then commenced in earnest and within the space of ten minutes several other parcels containing *disjecta membra* were recovered. They included other parts of the limb to which reference has been made and SECTIONS OF THE TORSO OF A WOMAN said to be of dark complexion and aged about thirty. Certain articles of clothing including a black sealskin jacket were also found and it is hoped that these may provide some further clue to the identity of the unfortunate woman. Although digging continued until late in the evening several parts of the corpse remain unaccounted for, including the head, the left arm and the right leg. The police surgeon is to make an examination today of the remains so far recovered and is expected to give an estimate of the height and physical proportions of the deceased, as well as the approximate time of death. Sergeant Cribb, meanwhile, appears to have made up his own mind about the latter by issuing a statement asking that anyone who saw a man and woman on the beach in the area of the fish market on Saturday night should report to the nearest police station. There are offices at the

Town Hall, Grafton Street, the Level, West Hill Road and
Preston. The investigation continues and a further report
will appear in our Saturday edition.

He folded the newspaper carefully, with the article
innermost, and set it beside him with two large pebbles
to anchor it. A third he kept in his hand, enjoying the feel
of its smooth, cool underside in his palm. The colour was
the bluish-grey that seemed to prevail in the shingle near
the West Pier. A white seam, marvellous in its precision,
bisected it. He turned the stone slowly, examining the surface for some flaw, but there was none. A perfect object in
an imperfect world. He rested it against his cheek and tried
to decide what he should do.

The subject of the newspaper article accounted for his
almost solitary occupation of the beach—or at least the
stretch of it between the two stone groynes. It was not that
people shunned the foreshore because of its association with
violence, nor that they paled at the prospect of what little
William might turn over with his wooden spade. Almost
the contrary. They were all at the fish market, watching
the comings and goings of the police, or filing through the
Aquarium for a peep at the crocodile tank. The public at
large had an insatiably morbid curiosity—so long as events
did not touch them personally.

A woman of about thirty, the newspapers said. Dark
complexion. Black sealskin jacket. It was not much to
go on, not the kind of description that settled anything,
although who was to say what the surgeon might discover
in his examination—some scar, perhaps, or a birthmark?

In cases of that sort, did the relatives of the deceased have memory or knowledge of such intimate details; weren't those the very blemishes a young woman sought to conceal from everyone—even her husband? Perhaps, after all, the remains would never be identified.

That was the curious thing about it: that the husband and son had not come forward to report her disappearance. How could anyone be so lacking in concern, so callous as to continue the holiday—the daily swim, the promenading, the visits to Lewes Crescent—as though nothing untoward had happened? If it were cruel to die, how infinitely more cruel when one's closest relatives appeared not to have noticed one's passing.

Going to the police would ruin the rest of his holiday, he knew. There would be difficult questions, statements to make, hours of waiting in police stations and later in the courts, notoriety of a sort—bad for business. Yet there was an inevitability about it all, a feeling that from the moment he had first brought her into focus he was no longer in control of events. So many things he had done since then had been contrary to all his practice, entirely out of character. Who would have thought a fortnight previously that he would today be sitting on a deserted beach actually *wanting* to be alone, when crowds—the exciting, inspiriting crowds he had never been able to resist—were massing in other parts of the town, a short walk away? No doubt about it: Zena Prothero had changed him fundamentally. Whatever the consequences, he owed it to her memory to answer Sergeant Cribb's appeal for assistance. There was no need to tell *everything;* simply enough to remove all doubts about her identity. He refused to allow her to become a 'person unknown,' a pen-stroke on a file at Scotland Yard. He got up decisively and flung the white-seamed pebble far into the waves. Then he picked up his newspaper, reminded himself of the address of the nearest police station, and started along the beach.

■ It was gratifying to discover that Sergeant Cribb was a sensitive listener, tolerant of others' little whimsies, not in the least disparaging about the optical experiments. The interview at Grafton Street lasted more than two hours and he was treated throughout with the utmost civility. He told the sergeant everything he thought he should know about Zena—of course, there were things one did not need to go into—even offering at the end to look at the severed hand, but Cribb explained that it was now in formalin and would be difficult to identify unless one were accustomed to such things.

'For the present,' said the sergeant, 'I'm quite content with the information you've volunteered, Mr. Moscrop. You don't mind if I go over one or two points again, so that Constable Thackeray here can check his notes?'

'Please do.'

'Very good, sir. The last time you saw Mrs. Prothero yourself was last Friday, when you met her by the croquet-lawn at the Albemarle to collect the sleeping-draught and get it analysed, is that correct, sir?'

'On Friday, yes.'

'And she seemed in good spirits then?'

'Oh yes. There was an air of conspiracy about the whole

thing which seemed to excite her. I found it rather taxing, myself.'

'She arranged to meet you outside the hotel the following evening, to get the results of the analysis?'

'Yes, at half past eight.'

'But you were met by Bridget, the maid, instead. What time was that?'

'Later. I remember looking at my watch. It was about nine o'clock. I had almost decided to leave.'

'You've got that, Thackeray?' said Cribb. 'And what did Bridget say about her mistress, Mr. Moscrop?'

'I understood that she was prevented from coming to meet me by her husband announcing that he was going out and insisting that she took her sleeping-draught before he went. However, she was reluctant to take the preparation without having seen the formula, so she pretended to have taken it—"foxed" was Bridget's expression, I remember— and feigned sleep when Dr. Prothero looked in on her. Of course, it was impossible afterwards, even though she was awake, to dress again in the short time remaining and come to meet me.'

'I can appreciate that, sir. So you gave the slip of paper with the formula on it to Bridget instead?'

'Yes. I explained that it was chloral hydrate she had been taking, and quite harmless. Then we were interrupted by the fireworks, I recall.'

'Ah yes. The night of the regiment's home-coming. There was a crowd to watch, I expect?'

'One soon materialised, Sergeant. People came from the hotels and lodging-houses and down the Old Steine to watch. Many were watching from the hotel balconies, young Guy Prothero included.'

'Not his stepmother, though.'

'No. She may have been watching from inside, however. Soon after that, Bridget left me to rejoin her and I made my way back along the front towards my lodgings.'

'You didn't stop to see the end of the fireworks, sir?'

'Pyrotechnics do not impress me over-much, Sergeant.'

'Nor me, sir. What time was it that you started your walk back?'

'About half past nine, I would estimate.'

'And when did you get back?'

'Oh, I cannot remember. Perhaps an hour later. I was in no hurry.'

'Possibly your landlady would recall?'

'Perhaps. No, I don't believe I saw her. I let myself in. I have a key, you know. Why are you interested?'

'I must get my times straight, sir. Sometimes it's crucial in a case like this, you know.' Cribb spoke with the air of a man imparting official secrets. 'A level-headed witness such as yourself can make all the difference when we're obliged to give evidence in court. There's a lot of reliance placed on times.'

'I'm quite sure.'

'Anyway, sir, you got back to the lodgings and went to bed. What happened next day?'

'It was Sunday, Sergeant. I went to church. I did not see the Protheros all day. I rather hoped that they might promenade or join the carriage parade after church, but I saw nothing of them. Nor was Zena—Mrs. Prothero, I should say—in her usual place on the beach the following day, although the weather was ideal. I did see the doctor on Monday, however, and in compromising circumstances which seemed not to perturb him one whit.'

'Really, sir? What was he doing?'

'Taking lunch at Mutton's with Miss Floyd-Whittingham, the young woman with copper-coloured hair. Afterwards they walked along the front to Lewes Crescent. Sergeant, they were arm in arm! It was as though he already knew—what we now know.'

'And you've seen him since then?'

'Several times. Twice with the young woman. Did you know that she is said to be a *colonel's* daughter? I would hazard that he spends each afternoon with her. His routine is inflexible, if my observations mean anything. He rises late, bathes at Brill's, has lunch at Mutton's or the Aquarium and then walks along the upper promenande to Lewes Crescent. Sometimes his son, Guy, has lunch with him.'

'What does the boy do with himself for the rest of the day?'

'He bicycles a good deal, and bathes.'

'What about the second son—the child?'

'Jason? I have seen nothing of him or his nursemaid since Saturday. Good God, Sergeant, the most appalling thought has occurred to me. You don't think—'

'No, sir, I don't. Not when I'm on a job like this. I just leave every possibility open. They *could* have been sent back to Dorking. One thing's certain—if you haven't seen 'em in four days they ain't in circulation here, we can depend upon it.'

He took the emphasis for a compliment. 'There isn't much that I miss, Sergeant. I shall naturally communicate everything else of significance that I observe. Dr. Prothero is still in ignorance of who I am, you see. My services as an observer are at Scotland Yard's disposal.'

Cribb coughed. 'Much appreciated, Mr. Moscrop, much appreciated. Now that you've given us this information, however, I think you're entitled to enjoy the rest of your holiday and leave the investigations to us. I'll get a statement of what you've told us neatly written out and I'd be obliged if you'd call in tomorrow to put your signature to it. Lovely sunshine outside, sir. Pleasant afternoon for a dip.'

CHAPTER 11

THE INCIDENT IN BRILL'S next morning was so alien to the good-humoured atmosphere traditionally engendered in swimming baths for gentlemen that everyone was caught unawares. Several patrons whose sorties from the side had them facing the wrong direction at the crucial moment frankly refused to believe that it had happened. Its onset was unimaginably sudden: a thrashing of water sufficient to suggest that a harpoonist had scored a hit near the centre of the pool, a frantic striking for the side, a cascading emergence of Dr. Prothero on the tiled surround, and an outraged challenge to the man standing in front of his changing-cubicle, 'That is my towel you are holding, sir!'

The defaulter, tall, sharp of feature, with a waspish look about him, not unconnected with the colours of his costume, said, 'No, sir. It is mine.'

'Good God!' said Prothero. 'I know my own towel. Return it to me at once, sir!'

The other unconcernedly applied the towel to his left arm-pit. 'You're mistaken. This is mine. I left it hanging over the cubicle door.'

Plainly shaken by the confidence of the performance, Prothero looked to right and left to get his bearings. 'But this is *my* cubicle and *my* green and white towel.'

'Perhaps your memory is at fault. Look around you. There are at least a dozen towels hanging over doors.'

'But none of them is green and white!' said Prothero, just refraining from stamping a bare foot.

'Exactly. You must have brought one of another colour with you. Easy to make mistakes about such unimportant things.'

Prothero stood like Alice in the presence of the Mad Hatter.

'If someone has taken yours,' the other advised him, 'we should tell the attendant. I could lend you this one, of course, but it's rather wet. Don't stand there getting cold. Walk around the edge of the pool at a sharp step and you'll be dry in no time. When I'm dressed I'll speak to the attendant for you. Things like this shouldn't be allowed to happen.' He towelled his hair vigorously. 'I don't know what Brill's is coming to when a man can't leave his towel hanging over a door without some scoundrel helping himself to it.'

'Would you believe me if my clothes were in the cubicle?' Prothero appealed. 'A silk hat and a frock-coat?'

'That's not all, I trust,' said the man with the towel, 'or

you *will* feel a draught. Certainly have a look. We're all liable to make mistakes. The door's unbolted, you see . . . Oh, my stars!'

'There!' said Prothero, vindicated by the contents of the cubicle. 'Now perhaps you will kindly return *my* towel.' The satisfaction of confounding such arrant self-righteousness quite made up for the state of the towel.

'How can I begin to apologise?' said the other. 'My own towel must have been taken—or did I leave it inside the cubicle? Good Lord, sir, I'm cut to the quick. Mortified with shame. It must be the circular shape of the building, you see. Lost my bearings.'

'It doesn't matter,' said Prothero loftily.

'But it does. The things I said. You must allow me to stand you a meal. If you don't, I shall never be able to hold my head up again.'

'It isn't necessary.'

'My name's Cribb. Shall we go to Mutton's?'

'Prothero—Dr. Prothero. There is really no need—'

'I'll find my cubicle and see you in a few minutes. The least I can do.'

So Sergeant Cribb presently sat with the doctor at a central table in Mutton's main dining-room, a monument to the glazier's craft, with mirrors along every wall, a domed skylight and chandelier above them and statuettes and wax flowers encased in glass on a buhl cabinet at one end. A third place was reserved for Prothero's son, after the doctor explained that they had arranged to meet there.

'There are just the two of you in Brighton, then?' Cribb ventured.

'Guy and myself, yes. My wife and younger son were here until Sunday, but they had to return to Dorking prematurely. The child was unwell.'

'I'm sorry to hear that. Some childish malady, I expect?'

'Oh, yes. I think the food upset him, or the change of air. He is not yet three. I told my wife to let the nursemaid take Jason home, but she was most insistent on going with them. It is her first child and she is devoted to it. Shall we order? Guy won't object, I'm sure. He is late, anyway—throwing an eye over the fillies in the King's Road, I shouldn't wonder. The two-legged ones. Are you here for the season, Mr. Cribb?'

'No, no. Business brings me to Brighton. What will you order, Doctor? I believe the turtle soup is just about obligatory.' When the waiter had gone, he said, 'I arrived here only two days ago. Missed the return of the regiment. Did you see them?'

'A stirring sight,' said Prothero. 'First-rate band, too. I don't think there was a soul left on the beach on the morning of the march-past. Are you a military man, Mr. Cribb? There's something of the soldier in your bearing.'

'Yes, I took the shilling in my time. Served a few years until the home comforts began to beckon. Did you get to the ball at the Dome? I suppose you wouldn't have been invited, not being resident in the town.'

'As a matter of fact, I was,' Prothero said, in a voice that suggested Cribb was making unwarranted assumptions again. 'It was the outstanding night of the season. *Everyone* was there.'

'How splendid! It must have made a fitting climax to your wife's holiday.'

'My wife was not present.'

'Oh. You took your son?'

'A friend. Guy has not enough manners yet for these occasions. My wife does not attend evening engagements for reasons of health. She is of a nervous disposition. Ah! Here comes the boy.' He signalled with a table-napkin. 'He's somewhat short on the social graces, Mr. Cribb, as you'll presently see. Had a rather narrow upbringing. I blame the school.'

Guy was wearing his red blazer. 'I thought we were taking lunch alone,' he told his father, with the merest glance at Cribb, who had stood to receive him.

'Mr. Cribb, this is my elder son, Guy.'

Cribb extended his hand. Guy produced his snuff and charged each nostril, ignoring the sergeant.

'Mr. Cribb met me in Brill's—'

'In circumstances too embarrassing to recall,' said Cribb, putting down his hand. 'I'm standing the lunch. Order whatever you wish.'

In a few minutes they were all busy with soup-spoons.

'Have you left school?' Cribb inquired conversationally.

'Ask him,' said Guy.

'It's a sensitive point at the moment,' Prothero explained. 'Guy has left one school and is about to start at another.'

'A boarding establishment?'

'Yes. This is by way of a farewell holiday. He starts in two weeks.'

'Where is the school?'

'He won't tell you where it is while I'm here,' Guy informed Cribb, ignoring his father. 'He doesn't want me to know. I'm treated no better than Jason. I'll have a sirloin steak next, cooked rare. It's probably in the Outer Hebrides.'

'Guy has a well-developed sense of humour which does not endear him to schoolmasters,' said Prothero. 'Or his family, on occasions.'

'It's true!' said Guy. 'When have you ever treated me with anything but suspicion? You're fearful all the time that I'll embarrass you and your quack theories. I can't even come on holiday without being forbidden to bathe in the sea because you think it's teeming with typhoid germs.'

'My quack theories, as you term them, are supported by a substantial correspondence in *The Lancet*, my boy,' retorted Prothero. 'Any other lad in your condition would be grateful that he had a doctor for a father. He suffers from asthma, you know,' he added, for Cribb's information, 'and I have made the disease my life's work. Don't so lightly dismiss the efforts I have made to alleviate your attacks, Guy.'

'How can I, when I have a bruise on my arm as big as half a crown to remind me? That's a father's loving care for you. I began to wheeze a bit on Sunday,' Guy told Cribb, 'so he gave me an injection of atropine. He might be a specialist on asthma, but he handles the needle like a punt-pole.'

'How long do you expect to be in Brighton, Mr. Cribb?' asked Prothero, in a way that indicated that so far as he was concerned the insults had gone far enough.

'Oh, as long as my business detains me.'

Guy turned sharply and looked at Cribb and then turned back to his father. 'What did you say his name was?' he asked.

'I told you,' said Prothero with a glare. 'This is Mr. Cribb.'

'I thought that was it! And you've only been in the town a day or two? You're the man from Scotland Yard, aren't you?' demanded Guy triumphantly. 'Investigating the body they dug up on the beach. I've read it in *The Argus*. What do they call you—*Inspector* Cribb?'

'Sergeant only, I'm afraid.'

'You'd better watch out, Father. Sergeant Cribb's looking for a murderer. Better get home quick and pour your poisons down the wash basin. Business! You're a fly one, Sergeant Cribb, aren't you?'

'It's never been the custom of detectives to give cards to everyone they meet,' said Cribb, matching the sarcasm. 'Perhaps you think I should give you an account, item by item, of what we uncovered the other morning. It's not my notion of lunch time conversation, but if you can enjoy a slice of sirloin at the same time, I'm sure I can. What would you like to know? Ah, here's the waiter. Are we all for steak, gentlemen?'

'I think the soup was quite sufficient,' said Prothero, palely.

'What about your son?'

Guy shook his head. 'I've changed my mind. I'll have a cold collation later.'

'Steak for one, then. Well done, if you please,' said Cribb. 'As it happens, gentlemen, it's the victim I'm concerned to identify. I'll find my murderer later. I want to know who the unfortunate woman was. There isn't much to go on, you see. Dark hair. Age about thirty. Small to medium height. Slim in build. Wearing a sealskin jacket and black skirt. Could be every other woman you pass in the street. That's why I have to know about women who haven't been seen in the town since Saturday—for whatever reason. It's my job to investigate every report.'

Prothero frowned. 'Am I to infer that you are concerned for the safety of my wife?'

'Yes, sir, since I have it on quite good authority that she hasn't been seen in Brighton since Saturday.'

There was a moment's uneasy silence.

'Your wife didn't accompany you to the ball,' Cribb added as if to strengthen the point.

The colour rose in the doctor's cheeks. 'I told you. She doesn't go out in the evening. She was in one piece on Sunday, dammit, and if you'd asked me in the first place I could have told you so.'

'You accompanied her to the station on Sunday morning?'

'Er—no. They took a cab.'

'Your wife, the maid Bridget and Jason?'

'Good God, man! Do you even know the name of my servant?'

'Did the three of them travel together, sir?' persisted Cribb.

'Naturally.'

'You saw them leave?'

'Of course! After a late breakfast. They would have caught the half past eleven train. If the change at Horsham didn't delay them, they must have been home by one.'

'That's good news, then,' said Cribb, leaning back in his seat as the steak was placed in front of him. 'Would you be so kind as to pass the French mustard? Whoever this young woman was, she was killed on Saturday night. Not far from your hotel, so you can understand my concern.'

'There were scores of men and women on the front that night,' Guy suddenly said. 'It was the firework show. I saw them from the hotel window. I expect a soldier got too much drink inside him and killed the doxy he was with. Then he dragged her into one of the lock-ups under the arches and left her until the next night, then he came back and set to work with the cleaver. There! I've solved the case for you.'

'It's one possibility,' said Cribb, without much gratitude. 'You say you watched the fireworks from the hotel. Were you with your stepmother?'

'She was asleep,' Prothero stated confidently.

'No, Father. She got up to watch the fireworks.'

'But she had taken her usual sleeping draught.'

'I think not. We watched the show together from your bedroom. She would tell you herself if she were here. I went out on the balcony for a time, but she was wearing her peignoir, so she remained inside.'

'The suite overlooks the front, I gather,' said Cribb.

'That's so,' Prothero confirmed. 'My wife and I have a double room with a balcony, the best in the hotel. Jason sleeps next door—or did until Sunday—with Bridget, and their window looks on to the sea, too. Guy is on the other side of the building, across the corridor. The boy's right, Mr. Cribb. There are always people along the front at night, and on the beach. Soldiers, sailors, silly little sluts of shop-girls and females of a certain profession. They don't go there just to promenade, I promise you. Brighton is not all it seems by day in the King's Road, you know. One has only to see the colonnade of the Theatre Royal between eleven and midnight—a veritable Gomorrah. The women of the town flock there from their sordid houses of assignation in Church Street and Edward Street and some do not even have the decency to take their clients back there. The Pavilion grounds aren't fit to walk through by night, and you may ask your friends at Brighton police station to verify that, if you wish.'

'I'm sure I shan't need to, sir. Now, gentlemen, the pastries here are recommended, I believe. Cooked on the premises. You'll have one on Scotland Yard, I hope, seeing that you haven't eaten very much.'

Guy stood up suddenly and tossed his crumpled napkin on the table. 'I don't want pastries. I need some fresh air.'

'His condition,' Prothero explained by way of an excuse, after the red blazer was lost to view. 'It's in the blood, inherited from his late mother. Providentially, I am able to subdue the attacks if I cannot dispel them altogether. I *will* have a pastry, if you please.'

The tray was brought and coffee served at the same time.

'I should think you've had your difficulties with Guy, then,' said Cribb.

'In which way, exactly?'

'Oh, I was meaning that it's difficult to correct a child when it's liable to bring on an attack of asthma.'

'Less difficult than you would suppose,' said Prothero defensively. 'I'll allow that he has abominable manners, but he's been chastised like any normal boy. We've done all that Christian parents can.'

'Perhaps the school was negligent,' ventured Cribb. 'You mentioned that he is starting at a new one.'

'Quite soon, yes.'

'I wonder if I've heard of it.'

'I shouldn't think so. A small private academy. There is still some doubt whether he will go there, so there is no point in my mentioning the name.' The subject was obviously closed.

'I didn't wish to be indiscreet when the boy was here,' said Cribb, 'but you won't mind if I now enquire whether it was a lady-friend you accompanied to the homecoming ball?'

'I fail to see what relevance it has to your investigation, but I am not ashamed to tell you I was partnering Miss Samantha Floyd-Whittingham, who happens to be the daughter of a senior officer of the regiment. She is purely a social acquaintance.'

'Goes without saying, sir. You didn't by any chance leave the ball for a part of the evening, perhaps to watch the fireworks?'

'Indeed, yes. Most of the guests did. We stood in the Steine Gardens for twenty minutes or so. We could see sufficiently well from there.'

'And then you returned inside, sir?'

'Of course, until the ball ended, soon after one o'clock. Then I drove the young lady to her lodgings in Lewes Crescent and returned to the Albemarle. I was home before two.'

'I don't doubt it, sir.'

'Samantha is still alive, I assure you. I saw her yesterday.'

'I wasn't thinking she was dead,' said Cribb.

'Oh. You are concerned about my *wife's* safety, but not about my—er—friend's?'

'Seeing that my information is that your friend has copper-coloured hair and the dead woman's is brown, that's correct, sir. There's just one other matter, if you'll indulge me a moment more. You've been most forbearing, if I might say so. Has your servant Bridget been with you long?'

'Upwards of six months, I believe. I engaged her myself. She has impeccable references. My wife has never been entirely happy with her, but I think the fault may well rest more with Mrs. Prothero than with Bridget.'

'What do you mean, sir?'

'She is far too possessive with the child. If you engage a nurse, you should let her get on with the job, dammit, not interfere at every opportunity. Mrs. Prothero is a woman of excitable tendencies, as I think I mentioned. It is usually a relief to all of us when she takes her sleeping-draught and retires. A profound relief. You may imagine the scenes we have had between my wife and Guy.'

'Vividly, sir. Do you think Bridget is completely to be trusted?'

'In what way?'

'Well, sir, not to put too fine a point upon it, in matters of morality.'

Prothero put down his coffee cup. 'My goodness, Sergeant Cribb, you *have* been making a close study of us. I am well aware to what you are alluding. You may think me a forward thinker in this respect, but I don't regard it as necessarily bad if a fifteen-year-old boy is taught a trick or two by a servant-wench. I know that I was when I was young. Oh yes, they bathe together. I don't need Scotland Yard to tell me what two wet bathing-costumes mean. But I tell you that I'm more concerned about the toxic effects of the sea-water than I am about a bit of spooning under the waves. There's no more to it than that, Sergeant. Bridget's no youngster.

She's not the sort to make a fool of herself with a schoolboy, but if she feels disposed to further his education a little in that direction, I shan't turn her out of the house for it. Guy might appear to be worldly-wise, with his scant respect for his elders and betters, but his knowledge of certain areas of human behaviour is not much better than your eye for a bath towel.' He wiped his lips thoughtfully, as if reconsidering what he had just said. 'I didn't notice whether your towel *was* green and white. I rather suspect now that it was not. Do you have it with you?'

'No sir,' Cribb was quick to reply. 'It was hired from Brill's.'

'And you're saying no more than that, eh? Well, Sergeant, I don't want you to think I'm ungrateful for the lunch, *whatever* occasioned it. I just hope for your sake that Scotland Yard will not consider it as unjustified expenditure.'

'If you are thinking of leaving, I'll accompany you as far as Grafton Street,' said Cribb as if he were bestowing a favour. 'You *were* going in the general direction of Lewes Crescent, I take it?'

Prothero stood up. 'Sergeant, it's a good thing I haven't done anything criminal, or I should be a worried man by now. By all means let's go together.'

Constable Thackeray was waiting with a letter in his hand when Cribb re-entered the police station. 'Blimey, Sarge, what have you done to yourself?'

'What do you mean?'

'There's something different about you and I'm not sure what it is. Yes I am! It's your hair.'

'What's the matter with it, for Heaven's sake?' growled Cribb.

'Well, it's standing up so, Sarge. You always have it plastered down. If I didn't know you'd been out interviewing I'd almost think you'd been in for a dip. It must be the sea air. I believe the ozone does things like that. You'll need to get some macassar-oil.'

There was a moment of silence before Cribb asked, 'Is that all, Constable, or would you like to inspect my tongue to see whether I'm becoming constipated? Shall we concern ourselves with the purpose of our visit? What have you got there?'

'It's the police surgeon's report, Sarge. I knew you'd want to open it yourself.'

Cribb opened the envelope and scanned its contents.

'Does it tell us anything new?' Thackeray asked.

'Precious little, so far as I can see. Merely cloaks our own observations in pathological jargon. He hasn't been able to establish a cause of death. *"In my opinion the deceased was a healthy woman aged between twenty-five and forty*—that's a sizeable margin. *Slight of build. Dark hair"*—we know all this. Ah! Here's a point of interest. *"The dismemberment of the parts was performed with a sharp axe-like instrument employed somewhat crudely. The state of coagulation suggests that the amputations took place up to twenty-four hours after death."* It looks as if our murderer killed the woman on Saturday, hid the body under the arches and returned to finish his work the next night.'

Thackeray lifted two scandalised eyebrows. 'On a *Sunday?*'

'My guess is that he wrapped the dismembered parts in newspaper and buried them a foot or so under the pebbles that night, thinking to come back.'

'He was taking a risk, Sarge, leaving them on a public beach. Just suppose a child had decided to dig there. It's unthinkable!'

Cribb shook his head. 'And unlikely. It's the site of the fish-market. Nobody sits down *there* with a child. The smell's too strong. Our murderer's a very knowing cove, I'd say, and a cool'un, too. When do you think the hand was deposited in the crocodile tank?'

'First thing in the morning, as soon as the aquarium opened, I should say. He probably had some of his grue-some parcels in a bag of some sort and got into the reptile-cave before anyone else and tossed them over the top.'

Cribb was unconvinced. 'I know that crocs are notorious flesh-eaters and scavengers, but it's asking the devil of a lot to expect 'em to finish everything before the first visitors arrive. That cave's a popular place, you know.'

'The hand *was* found in the morning,' protested Thackeray.

'Only because it slipped between the rock and the glass. No, I think it's far more likely he got in there by night.'

'Broke in, d'you mean?'

'Why not? It's just a short step from where the parts were buried.'

'He'd have to be a skilled cracksman as well as a killer to do that Sarge.'

'Not at all. You haven't studied the lay of the building, I can see, in spite of walking past it two or three times a day. What's its situation?'

'Well, it stands between the upper promenade and the lower,' said Thackeray, increasingly peeved at Cribb's manner. 'In the fork of Madeira Drive and the Marine Parade.'

'Correct. And one being on a higher level than the other, what's the effect on the siting of the building?'

'It's built hard against the rise of the upper promenade. The roof is on a level with the Marine Parade. They've made a terrace garden there.'

'Exactly! You can walk on the roof. Hundreds of people do without realising it. But if you've got a sharp eye,' (the implication plainly was that Thackeray had not), 'and you take a look over the balustrades and under ledges you'll see windows, dozens of 'em. They're needed at the top to let the condensation out. Now it's perfectly evident to anyone who walks along there that not all of those windows are closed at night. And it wouldn't need a Charlie Peace to let himself in through one. It's no great height, and some of the windows must be positioned over beams and furniture. I think he got in there by night. That's probably why his aim with the hand wasn't too good.'

'Wouldn't he have risked being seen breaking in?'

'Hardly any risk at all if he worked from the side nearest the Parade. There's a kind of well at one point between the building and the road. You can't see into it unless you stand against the railing and lean over. That's where *I'd* make my entry. I'm having one of the local detectives examine the windows there for marks. Well, there's not much more in this report. How did you get on this morning?'

Thackeray mopped his brow with a large handkerchief. 'This list you asked me to make is getting longer, Sarge. The Brighton bobbies are doing the door to door work, but I'm kept quite busy taking reports from them. There's more than a hundred women on it already, and it's the deuce of a job to discover what their age was. They all left the town on Saturday or Sunday, though. Finished their holidays, you see. I'm beginning to understand what attracts a murderer to a seaside resort. Oh, and the man Moscrop called again.'

'What did he want?'

'He asked to see you. It seems he remembered something that might be of vital importance. He wanted to look at the sealskin jacket we found, but I didn't let him, of course. I tried to explain that it was evidence and that if he became a witness he might be called upon to identify the coat in court, and—'

'What did he say about the coat?' demanded Cribb.

'Oh it was something to do with a missing button. While Mrs. Prothero was walking along the prom. with him, a button came off her jacket. She put it in her pocket. I think he was hoping to identify the jacket we found by locating the button in the pocket, but I was able to tell him that the buttons was all in place, and we hadn't found nothing in the pockets. He went away after that.'

'Did he say which button was missing?' asked Cribb.

'The top one.'

'Fetch the coat.'

'You won't find the button gone, Sarge,' mumbled Thackeray, as he went to collect it. 'I checked it again myself after he'd gone. But if you won't take my word for it . . .'

In a moment he returned with the jacket and planted it on the table in front of Cribb with a sigh pregnant with injured pride. Cribb examined each button carefully. 'Hand me that magnifying-glass, Constable.' He turned the buttons back and studied the cotton-strands holding them in place. 'Interesting. The top button's sewn on with thinner cotton than the rest, but there's still traces of the holes where the thicker stuff went through. Someone's had to sew the button on again. I rather think that Moscrop's come to your rescue, Thackeray. You needn't do any more work on that list. He's found the lady for us.'

CHAPTER

12

MOSCROP SAT ON THE sea-wall that extended from the Junction Road past the aquarium to the Chain Pier. The position was well-chosen. It commanded a clear view of the front of the Albemarle Hotel from the lower road, without the obvious risk involved in watching from the Marine Parade itself. He could sit here inconspicuously for as long as he liked, pretending to contemplate the symmetry of the structure suspended over the sea between the four tapering towers inspired by the Egyptian architects of Karnak—for the Chain Pier still had its admirers, even if it lacked the amusements of its more fashionable rival farther up the shore-line. Today its clientele were mostly anglers, with some few promenaders tossing halfpennies into the shallows to see the local urchins scramble for them. People said that Tom Sayers, the great pugilist, was once one of these 'Jacks in the water.'

It was difficult to credit that an incomparable woman had

been murdered and dismembered on this beach just a day or two earlier. The town had taken account of the crime and recorded it in its newspapers like one of the events of the season and now it was forgotten, a horror swept clean by the tides, and crushed out of reckoning by the implacable round of promenading, carriage-exercise, concert-going and 'at homes.' Landladies were haggling over the price of cod where the day before yesterday policemen and auxiliaries had dug for human remains. Today's newspapers were full of the Grand Temperance Demonstration by the Band of Hope Union.

He, for one—perhaps the only one in Brighton—refused to forget what had happened and return to the bucket and spade level of existence. It was not the holiday he had planned, this furtive waiting and watching, not quite the scintillating drawing-room exchanges with the season's gayest debutantes that he had visualised in his most extravagant moments. But if it had not come up to *those* expectations, it had touched planes of experience he had not dared to contemplate before. They had been momentous, those few meetings with Zena, transforming him utterly, making poor faded cameos of the sights he had caught through his instruments in years past and treasured in his mind's eye. Now that it was over he was not going to behave as though nothing had happened. Nor would he slink dispiritedly away. He would see things through, watch the sequence of events, patiently observe as he had always done.

It was not all observation, even now. Anyone who had been so involved in events was entitled to bring a little influence to bear on the way they were interpreted. That was why he had gone to the police about the matter of the coat-button. What a pity it was that he had been attended to by the constable, and not his shrewd superior! The man seemed positively pleased to report that all the buttons on the sealskin coat were in position, planting his hands across his belly like some smug grocer promising a customer that all the eggs in his shop were new-laid. One could not even be sure he would mention the matter to Sergeant Cribb, who could be relied upon to understand its significance and employ the resources of Scotland Yard to establish that the button in question had been replaced recently. *'Extensive inquiries are afoot.'* the newspapers were saying, as though that ought to satisfy everyone. Such complacency! How was one to convince these policemen that there was no need to tramp from door to door asking questions about missing women?

The present necessity was to watch every move that Dr. Prothero made. Sooner or later the investigation must concentrate on him. The circumstantial evidence was overwhelming. Here was a man who had already buried two wives and was treating his third as though she did not exist, openly deserting her by day and administering chloral to her by night to keep her in ignorance of his iniquitous infidelities. Zena herself had described the marriage as 'a continuous ordeal' and talked of the 'unspeakable thing' that made the child Jason her single consolation. Cribb had made a note of the phrases when they were repeated to him and could be relied upon to understand their significance. Oh no, it would not be long before Dr. Prothero came under suspicion for the murder of his wife. Wasn't membership of the medical profession tantamount to a predisposition for murder? There was a long line of murderous doctors, from Palmer, the Rugeley poisoner, to George Henry Lamson, who had gone to the gallows as recently as April for killing his crippled brother-in-law. Doctors had the means of disposal to hand, after all, and their work brought them into such intimate contact with death that it was no surprise if occasionally one of them developed a cynical indifference to it, even a predilection for it as a convenient way of solving problems. Palmer and his kind were those who had made errors. How many others in the same profession had committed similar crimes nobody had detected?

The details of the case—the circumstances in which Prothero had returned from the regimental ball and Zena had been on the beach—were for Scotland Yard to determine. What mattered was that until they were ready to arrest the doctor every move he made should be observed, every suspicious action recorded, and he, Moscrop, would see that it was done. A singular way to pass a holiday, but one that, curiously enough, brought him peace of mind.

Beyond the barques and pleasure-yachts dotting the expanse of the sea, a war vessel was at gun-practice, a compelling spectacle, for after each flash on the water and before the puff of white smoke dispersed, there was a moment's hiatus while one waited for the boom of the gun. He was watching this phenomenon for perhaps the fifth time and beginning to speculate more generally on the delay between cause and effect when he saw that Dr. Prothero had come down the steps of the Albemarle and was turning into the Marine Parade in the direction of the Aquarium. That he was not going to look at fish or reptiles this morning was evident from his clothes. He wore walking-boots and leggings and carried a stick and a bulky knapsack. His stride bore all the indications of a long hike in prospect.

Moscrop pulled nervously at the ends of his moustache. This was a new development, quite foreign to the routine of Brill's, Mutton's and Lewes Crescent that he had thought was inflexibly established. It held him temporarily incapable of action. Anything else—a carriage-drive, a boat-trip, a walk along the pier—he could reasonably have accepted. But this—it was unaccountable, and quite impossible to have anticipated. Heavens! Where was the man going dressed like that, striding towards the centre of town?

He set off numbly in pursuit, through Steine Gardens and past the Victoria fountain, forced almost into a trotting gait to keep within sight of the eccentrically dressed doctor, who was passing with his knapsack—who would credit it? under the very shadow of the Town Hall towards North Street. The trail continued past the circulating libraries, Treacher's and Wright's, across the junction with West Street and into Dyke Road, the steep ascent making no appreciable difference to Prothero's rate of progress.

Moscrop had reason to be thankful for his daily constitutional along Oxford Street; Prothero was demonstrably in better physical condition than men half his age. But the necessity of keeping pace was not the most alarming aspect of the march. Of more concern to Moscrop was the grim sense of purpose in the set of the doctor's shoulders and the almost military rigidity of his head. This was no taking of the air; it was a calculated march and it was leading them by the quickest possible route to one of the highest points of the South Downs. The knapsack, boots and leggings, so out of place among the shoppers in North Street, were entirely justified here, and Moscrop, in canvas shoes and flannels, was pathetically ill-equipped. Aside from the folly of attempting to cover uneven terrain in such gear, he faced the prospect of appearing as conspicuous on the Downs as Prothero had looked in Brighton.

As they approached Seven Dials he made the decision he knew he must: he would watch Prothero cross the road, see which route he took of the half-dozen available, and then double back to his lodgings for his walking boots and the Zeiss binoculars, staking the power of the lens on the open slopes against the twenty minutes start he would thereby sacrifice. If, as he suspected, Prothero had decided for his own reasons to walk clean out of Brighton and over the Downs by the loneliest route, someone must give pursuit. The man might never be heard of again. It would be a grave mistake to depend upon young Guy to lead the authorities to his father. The boy had left the Albemarle half an hour before Dr. Prothero that morning, and in all probability was already pedalling out of Brighton along some quiet lane on a hired bicycle.

At the Seven Dials crossroad, Prothero marched unhesitatingly to the continuation of Dyke Road. Moscrop turned left into Vernon Terrace and unashamedly ran down the hill towards his lodgings.

■ One of the largest of the arch-fronted buildings under the Parade had been put at Constable Thackeray's disposal. So had Constable Murphy, principally known in Brighton for his tea-making. Unhappily, no one had provided a gas-ring.

'I could always try the boxing saloon next door,' suggested Murphy. 'It's known locally as the Blood Hole but I reckon the owners might try to think of something else after this week's melancholy happenings. Sugar and milk for you?'

'We'll leave it for half an hour, shall we?' said Thackeray. 'We should be through this lot by then and I'll enjoy one of your specials back at Grafton Street when I've got the smell of fish off my hands. Found anything else in your bin?'

'It's mainly driftwood and seaweed,' said Murphy.

'Lay it all out neat, just the same. Those was the sergeant's orders.'

The floor was already three-parts covered with objects taken from the beach during the diggings earlier in the week. In the search for human remains everything picked up except pebbles had been deposited in bins. The necessary work of sifting the contents for a possible clue was in the capable hands of Thackeray and Murphy.

'Your sergeant's taken the afternoon off, has he?' said Murphy, carefully smoothing out a strip of seaweed and placing it, like a necktie, over the back of a convenient chair.

'I don't think he'd do that,' said Thackeray. 'He's not above fitting in a swim now and then, but he wouldn't take long over it. No, he's gone to Dorking on the train, as a matter of fact. Pursuing inquiries there. No offence intended towards you, of course, but I wouldn't mind being with him. I think he might have something to say to the newspapers when he gets back tonight.'

'What's that—the name of the murdered woman?'

'I ain't at liberty to say,' said Thackeray primly. 'Hey! Keep your eyes on the job. That's a piece of paper you've got there. All the paper has to come to me. Sergeant Cribb's instructions.'

The instructions (which Murphy could not very well dispute, Cribb having communicated them through Thackeray) were that Thackeray should take charge of anything made of paper, cloth and metal, while Murphy handled the rest, including seaweed, driftwood, gull's feathers and fish remains.

'Here's another garter for you, anyway,' said Murphy. 'That's the fifth, and they're all too faded to have been there just since Saturday. This old beach could tell a few stories—what's that you've got?'

Thackeray unfolded a piece of blue paper. 'I'm damned if it ain't the very thing the sergeant asked me to look for! This is going to make my day. Here. Come and have a look.'

The paper was headed 'Saddington and Sims. Dispensing Chemists.' The words written on it had become smudged from exposure to the damp, but they were clearly legible.

3rd October, 1882

'To Mr. A. Moscrop.

Our analysis of the liquid you brought in yesterday morning shows it to be a weak solution of chloral hydrate (CCL3 CH 20H). The charge is two shillings and sixpence.'

'He said it would be here somewhere,' said Thackeray. 'Oh, he's a leary old cove, is my sergeant.'

'How did he reason it out, then?' asked Murphy, not without a tinge of scepticism.

'He didn't say, but it's obvious enough—if you've done a bit of detective work before. Mrs. Prothero asked this man Moscrop to get her sleeping-potion analysed to see what her husband was dosing her with, d'you see? Her maid collected it from Moscrop and took it to her. Now when she goes off along the beach and gets murdered, she's going to have it on her person, ain't she? She ain't so daft as to leave it in the hotel-room where her husband might pick it up.'

'Clever,' said Murphy, genuinely impressed. 'I've got another question for you now. How did Mrs. Prothero come to be on the beach on Saturday night?'

'Now that's something Cribb and I are working on,' said Thackeray, leaning forward across his bin. 'Her husband thought she was already drugged with chloral and asleep, but we know she was awake. We've got two people's word for that—Bridget, the maid, told Mr. Moscrop, and young Guy told the sergeant. So there was nothing to stop her from putting on her clothes and going out.'

'The others would have noticed,' said Murphy.

'Perhaps they did. Nobody's asked 'em yet. She could have slipped out while they was on the balcony watching the fireworks.'

'Why would she want to go out?'

'It seems to me that there's two possible answers to that question,' said Thackeray, prodding the air magisterially with a wooden spade. 'Either she thought she would go down and see if her husband was among the crowd watching the fireworks, or she had decided after all to thank Mr. Moscrop for bringing the good news about the chloral.'

'And then someone murdered her,' said Murphy. 'It's a pestiferous quarter at night, is Brighton beach. No place for a respectable married lady. It could be one of hundreds that struck her down. I don't envy you, trying to find the one that did it.'

'It *could* be a total stranger, I grant you,' said Thackeray, 'but something tells me it ain't. It would help if we knew how she was killed, but the police surgeon wasn't very helpful on that point. All he'll say is that the tests he has made show her to have been in good health. It's a crying shame we didn't recover all of the parts.'

'We haven't even found all the clothes,' said Murphy, 'unless there's something in that pile of yours. What about her shoes, for example? There isn't a shoe among this lot.'

'I wasn't expecting to find any,' said Thackeray. 'Shoes are very significant things. We can tell a lot from a shoe at the Yard. I reckon myself that the killer realised how much they give away and carried 'em as far from the scene of the crime as he could. And some of the clothes, too. He probably had a bag of some sort, and stuffed everything in that would go. The jacket and skirt, being larger than the rest, had to be left behind. No, we won't find any more of her clothes than we've got already. This piece of paper is the most important thing. How about that cup of tea?'

▪ In other circumstances the long ascent of Dyke Road on to the Downs would have enraptured a man equipped (as

Moscrop now was) with a powerful pair of binoculars. The views of the town behind him and the sea beyond, of Hove, Kingston, Shoreham and the mouth of the river Adur had him feeling for the buckle-straps of his instrument-case repeatedly, only to check himself with the thought that there could be just one subject for study that afternoon. It was essential that he gave himself absolutely to the task of spotting Dr. Prothero on the slopes ahead.

Soon after sighting Patcham windmill (he was grateful for the map he had snatched from his landlady's hallstand drawer) he reached the top of a ridge where the road forked and a sign indicated the way to Poynings. Saddlescombe, a small village in a hollow half hidden by trees, lay below, but he elected to continue along the Dyke Road, reasoning to himself that it was wise to gain height by the quickest route. Prothero had still been walking at a sharp step when he had last seen him an hour before, and he doubted whether it was possible to win back much of the ground between them, but there was the massive expanse of downland ahead, with only low bushes intervening. The glasses would be a potent ally up there. He would reach the brow, some seven hundred feet above sea level, and then sweep the landscape repeatedly. Until he reached there, the prospect of recognising anyone at such a distance was remote. If he got the glasses out for a moving figure it was ten to one that it would be a grazing sheep.

He completed the final ascent to the ancient wind-swept hill-camp forming the summit of the Downs at this point and sat to recover his breath in a clump of long ur-grass the sheep had left. The range of vision on every side was now so vast and the panorama so intricately varied that it could well take an hour's work with the binoculars to isolate a single moving figure. He would need to stake everything on Prothero still being somewhere on the Down. The foot of the escarpment that had come so suddenly into view as he reached the top, dipping sheerly ahead into the vast plain of the Weald, was rich with autumn foliage—unbelievably beautiful in the afternoon sun, but making it well-nigh impossible to track a man with binoculars.

He took out the Zeiss and cast about to decide which direction was the most promising. To the west, on the brow of Fulking Hill, a mile or so distant, he fancied he could see a movement. He trained the glasses in that direction, first finding the prominent circle of beeches known as Chanctonbury Ring, altogether too distant. A small inclination to the left and a delicate movement of the screw-focus gave him what he wanted. There was a figure, human and moving—but mounted. He let the glasses drop.

Below and to his right more figures were positioned on either side of the Devil's Dyke, the spectacular gash in the hillside from which the long road up from Brighton took its name. For some reason he had not remembered its existence until this moment, in spite of having toiled up Dyke Road for more than an hour. He had read all about it in the gazetteer, in the train, two Saturdays ago. So recent as that? Unbelievable. At any rate, legend said that the Devil cut the cleft through the chalk with the object of letting in the sea to flood the churches in the Weald. Certainly it had a devilish look to it from this view, with its steeply sloping sides a thousand feet apart, faced with smooth turf. A small hotel on the near side bore witness to the Dyke's popularity with excursionists from the town.

He now began systematically examining through the binoculars the people in view on either side of the ravine, eliminating women and children at a glance, but several times finding himself compelled to wait for a man to turn his face out of shadow, and then being disappointed. Then, when he was ready to believe his wily quarry had somehow escaped, the glasses picked out a fawn-coloured object on the far side of the Dyke. The knapsack. And as the field of view moved left, he saw Dr. Prothero standing and staring at something, shading his eyes with both hands.

For a moment he had the uncomfortable feeling that the doctor was looking straight at him. As he put the glasses embarrassedly down, he realised how impossible it was. Besides, Prothero had no reason to suspect he was being followed.

What was he looking at, then? A landmark, most likely. He was taking his bearings before moving on. Away to the north was the blue mound of Leith Hill, beyond which was Dorking. Was that where he was making for? It was twenty-five miles away, six or seven hours of walking, even at Prothero's sprightly step.

He put the glasses to his eyes again and as he did so Prothero picked up the knapsack and began walking back in the general direction of the road, still looking anxiously about him as though he were expecting to see something or somebody he had not found. Some fifty yards on, he stopped, produced a white handkerchief and began waving it energetically. In an agony of curiosity, Moscrop dared not move the binoculars off him to see the recipient of the signal. Soon it was obvious that Prothero, now picking his way quickly up the slope, the knapsack fairly bouncing on his back, had established some kind of contact. There was not long to wait. Near the top of the slope, Prothero was joined in the field of view by a woman on horseback, quite probably the rider Moscrop had first seen on Fulking Hill. The doctor helped her dismount and then took her arm as they walked with the horse over the brow of the hill towards Saddlescombe.

So that was it. An assignation. It was too indiscreet now to meet on the promenade in front of Lewes Crescent, so they were using the Dyke for a rendezvous, going by separate routes in order not to arouse suspicion.

He lifted the binocular-strap over his head and clapped the glasses back into their case. An assignation. It was more than a little disappointing. He had been ready to take up the trail all the way to Dorking, through the night, if necessary. Now there was nothing to tell the police that they did not know already. They were not going to be interested *where* Prothero met his mistress.

Nor would he demean himself by following them any further. Their squalid embraces were beneath contempt.

He took out the map. There was an inn marked at the village of Poynings, down the hill. He would take the road that way and fortify himself with a lemon shandy. Perhaps two.

Some fifteen minutes later, as he passed down and among the trees, the sounds of late afternoon reasserted themselves after the rush of wind against his ears on the higher slopes.

Sheep-bells chinked nearby with their flat, but comforting note, and from behind he heard hooves on the road, jarring heavily, taking the strain of horse and rider down the steep incline. Automatically, he moved to the verge and waited to let them pass. It was a lady rider, the same he had seen with Prothero. She was alone now. The sun from over her shoulder prevented him from seeing her face clearly, but as she approached she called out to him.

'Good Lord, darling! What are you doing in this Godforsaken place? You ought to be on Brighton promenade.'

There was no mistaking the voice. The woman was Zena.

13

'YOU'LL PARDON ME IF I continue with my supper?' said Sergeant Cribb. 'All I had today was something alleged to be a ploughman's lunch. Ploughman! I wouldn't have offered it to a jockey on Derby Day. What have you got to tell me this time, Mr. Moscrop?'

He was installed at a corner table in the bar-parlour of *The Seven Stars* in Ship Street, a pint of East India and a large meat pie in front of him.

'I would not presume to disturb your meal if it were not a matter of paramount importance,' Moscrop began. 'You see, I have seen Mrs. Prothero!'

Cribb said nothing. His jaws continued to work at the meat pie.

'Mrs. Prothero,' repeated Moscrop with emphasis. 'She was at the Devil's Dyke this afternoon. I have come to you direct from seeing her.'

'Have you now?' said Cribb. 'You'll be hungry then. That's no end of a walk. Would you like me to order a pie?'

'Sergeant, I don't know whether you heard. It was Mrs. Prothero, alive and well. There can be no mistake. I spoke to her myself.'

'Did you, indeed?' said Cribb. 'You were luckier than I was, then. I went to Dorking on a similar mission.'

'You? To Dorking? Do you mean that you *knew* she was alive?'

'"Knew" is putting it a trifle strong, sir. One can never be sure if anyone is still on his feet in this uncertain life, but I had reason to believe she might be, yes. What was she doing on the Dyke—meeting Prothero?'

Moscrop regarded Cribb with the look clairvoyants like to see on the faces of their clients.

'Perhaps you should give me your account of it,' said Cribb, 'beginning with your pursuit of Prothero—since I take it you didn't climb the Downs for reasons of health.'

In diminished tones, Moscrop described the events culminating in the appearance of Zena Prothero.

'She was surprised at seeing you, I expect?' said Cribb.

'No more than I was at seeing *her*. Sergeant, I was so sure that she was dead that I was quite unable to speak for several seconds. Then I managed to stammer something to the effect that I had been recommended to look at the view from the Dyke.'

'Resourceful. Did you ask what she was doing?'

'No need. She was quite candid, and not in the least embarrassed at meeting me. She has a rather individual turn of phrase, as I may have remarked—a tendency to address quite recent acquaintances in terms of endearment—'

'Really, sir? Perhaps you would give me an example.'

'Darling.'

'I beg your pardon.'

'Darling. She calls everyone darling, or some equivalent phrase.'

'A generous-hearted woman. And what *was* she doing on the Down?'

'She made no bones about it. She had come to meet her husband.'

'Ridden out from Dorking, d'you mean?' said Cribb, in disbelief.

'No, from Bramber, a railway station some six miles to the west of the Dyke. She had travelled there by train this morning and hired a horse to ride along the top of the Downs to meet Dr. Prothero.'

'Who arranged this meeting?'

'As I understand it, she did. She wrote to her husband explaining that young Jason had quite recovered from his indisposition—you will remember that it was because of this she took the child back to Dorking on Sunday—and that she wished to collect certain articles of dress she had left behind in her somewhat hurried departure. They were the contents of the knapsack he was carrying, you see.'

'So he handed it over when they met?' said Cribb.

'Yes. It was attached to the horse when I saw her. She was planning to return to Bramber along the road, not wishing to ride over the Downs in failing light, so she took the road down to Poynings, and that was where she overtook me. We talked as I accompanied her down the hill.'

'Did you tell her that you thought she was dead?'

'Indeed, yes,' said Moscrop earnestly. 'I felt obliged to, having behaved towards her as if she were an apparition when she first greeted me. It was her so sudden departure from Brighton that misled me, and I told her so.' He cleared his throat. 'I am afraid that I told her something else, Sergeant.'

'Oh. What was that?'

'Something I now discover to be a misrepresentation of the truth. I told her that the police also believed her to have—er—joined the choir invisible.'

'I'd call that jumping to conclusions, sir. What did she say to it?'

'That she had no idea her innocent action had led to such complications. She at once entreated me to assure you that I had seen her and she was alive and perfectly well. She said—I think I can remember her words—that she could not bear to think of those poor pets of policemen running about Brighton like beavers because of her.'

'Decent sentiment,' said Cribb, with a sniff. 'Did you ask her about the sealskin jacket we dug up?'

'The jacket? Why, no,' said Moscrop. 'It wasn't hers, was it? Your constable told me that all the buttons were in place. But I did succeed in convincing her that she had a public duty to present herself at a police station to show that she was alive. She said she would do better than that. She would come to Brighton again and meet you, since you are in charge of the inquiry.'

'Good. That'll save me from another ploughman's lunch in Dorking. When's she coming?'

'Tomorrow morning. She was intending anyway to go on to Worthing tonight, where she has a sister, and return to Dorking tomorrow. At my suggestion she will take the first passenger-steamer tomorrow morning, and I very much hope that you will be able to meet the *Brighton* when it docks at the West Pier soon after ten o'clock. I must explain, though, that she is most particular about not being seen in conversation with you. She is anxious not to discommode her husband, you understand.'

'Why should he feel discommoded if she talks to me?' asked Cribb.

'Ah. Well it seems that you made a not too favourable impression there, Sergeant, when you had lunch with Dr. Prothero at Mutton's. He must have given her an account of it, because she will only consent to see you if you go on board the *Brighton* while it is moored at the pier. She fears that in any other part of the town there is a risk of his seeing her in conversation with you.'

'A clandestine meeting, eh? You've got *me* at it now, Mr. Moscrop. And I suppose you'll need to be there to make the introductions. Very well, sir. Ten o'clock on the pier-head.'

■ Moscrop was there by half past nine, watching with the Zeiss for the line of dark smoke that would indicate the steamer's approach. The morning was cool, the sky flecked with thin cloud in a herring-bone pattern, the beach deserted except for fishermen and a few small boys armed hopefully with shrimping-nets. On the pier one received the inescapable impression of being an intruder, although the turnstile-man accepted the twopence readily enough. Brawny employees of the company, normally out of sight, were swabbing the decks in a perfunctory fashion and providing an exhibition of bare chests and braces. Moscrop was careful not to upset any of them by stepping on their work.

Sergeant Cribb, when he arrived fifteen minutes after, was less sensitive, planting his feet confidently on the wet planking, his lofty frame reflected under him. There was a man with style, Moscrop decided. No pier-hand would be so injudicious as to question *his* right to cross the boards.

'Fresh breeze this morning, Mr. Moscrop. There's a choppy look to that water. I hope the lady's a good sailor.'

By now the *Brighton* was well in view and steaming past Shoreham. 'Would you care to try the binoculars, Sergeant?'

'No thank you, sir. I've made it my practice to avoid using such things.'

'Really? I should have thought them an invaluable weapon for fighting crime.'

'In isolated cases, yes,' said Cribb. 'Most other times they're a perishing nuisance. A positive encouragement to crime.'

'Come, come, Sergeant. That sounds to me like a claim you cannot possibly substantiate. Which particular crime do you have in mind?'

'Dipping, sir.'

'Dipping?'

'Picking pockets. When a man's peering through those things, he's a perfect invitation to a dipper. I could have copped four or five of the locals at it this week alone if I hadn't had more important things to do. It's a seaside occupation. Make a count of your handkerchiefs when you get home. Then you'll know if I'm exaggerating.'

They were joined at this point by several swarthy individuals in nautical clothes, ready for the steamer's arrival. Moscrop slipped the glasses quickly into their case. He would never be able to use them with the same confidence again.

Little more was said until the *Brighton* had berthed and a handful of passengers disembarked. Gulls screamed and swooped about the pier distractingly as Cribb and Moscrop descended the iron staircase to the landing stage. Words were exchanged with the white-capped man controlling the gangway, and they stepped across to the vessel itself.

'She'll be below,' Moscrop explained confidently.

She was, alone in the First Class Saloon, wearing a bottle-green coat in a military style and boots with 'fast' front lacings. Moscrop effected the introductions and stepped back.

'Handsome of you to come all this way to see me, Ma'am,' said Cribb.

'Oh, no. Handsome of *you*, Sergeant Cribb, to agree to see me on my own terms.' Under the rakishly-angled hat, which matched her coat in colour, her face was more pale than Moscrop remembered it, but the features just as exquisite. 'Particularly since I would seem to have put you to some trouble. Mr. Moscrop told me that you thought I was dead. I hope I can reassure you on that point.'

'Thank you, Ma'am. It *was* a bit of a puzzle to me when you left Brighton in such a hurry. The little boy was ill, I understand.'

'Jason? Yes. My husband decided that Brighton had upset him, so I took him back to Dorking on Sunday.'

'What was the matter with him exactly?'

'Oh, he was fretful the day before, you know, and awfully flushed. We thought he might have pains in his stomach. He has quite recovered now, the little beast. I wish you could see him. Mr. Moscrop is quite attached to Jason, aren't you, darling? But Scotland Yard didn't come to listen to a mother's doting nonsense, did it, Sergeant?'

Cribb took the cue. 'Might I trouble you about a few things just to set matters straight, Ma'am? I wonder whether you can recall how you spent last Saturday evening, your last night in Brighton.'

She put her hand to her forehead. 'Saturday evening? Good God! This is just like one of those novels from the circulating library. The characters always remember *exactly* what the policeman wants to hear.'

'It would have been your last night in Brighton, Ma'am,' Cribb prompted her.

'The night of the firework-display? Oh, yes, I shan't let you down after all. I have a clear recollection. All too embarrassing, now I come to talk about it. Mr. Moscrop and I had made a secret arrangement, hadn't we, my chuck? Being a man with scientific interests, you see, and an abso-lute Galahad to ladies in distress, he agreed to help me find out what my sleeping-potion consisted of, and took it to a chemist in Brighton. We arranged that he should bring me the answer and—well, you could tell Sergeant Cribb, your-self, couldn't you, darling?'

'I'd rather hear it from you, if you don't mind, Ma'am,' said Cribb quickly.

'Very well.' She shrugged. 'There's precious little to tell. Prothero, my husband, decided to go out for the evening, and was most particular about my being in bed before he went. I'm inclined to be nervous, you see.'

'I hadn't noticed it, Ma'am.'

'How gallant! So I retired before Prothero left and pre-tended to have taken my sleeping-potion. That was unfor-tunate, really, because being in my night-things I could not possibly meet my knight in shining armour, Mr. Moscrop. I had to send my nursemaid, Bridget, instead. It must have seemed monstrously ungrateful.'

'Not at all,' murmured Moscrop.

'Then the fireworks began. Oh, awfully exciting, and almost in front of the hotel! We had a grandstand position. Such fireworks, too! Sky-rockets and Catherine wheels and Chinese crackers. Set-pieces in tribute to the regiment, her Majesty's head in profile and a crocodile, to represent Egypt, you know!'

'I remember that,' said Moscrop.

'That would be after Bridget had left you, would it?' asked Cribb, suddenly addressing a question to him.

'Er—yes. I had given her the formula and I was starting to return along the front. I don't believe I saw all of the display.'

'So Bridget came back to you while the fireworks were still on?' said Cribb, switching back to Zena.

'Yes, and then I gave her the rest of the evening off, to watch the display. She was most excited about the sky-rockets. I was not left alone, you see. I had Guy with me throughout the evening. We watched from my bedroom window. Guy stood on the balcony for a time.'

'I saw him there,' said Moscrop helpfully.

'How long did the display continue after Bridget went out again?' asked Cribb.

'Oh God! You do ask some questions! Let me see. Half an hour, at least.'

'Then you went to bed?'

'No, I played cards with Guy for an hour. I've taught the little fiend to play cribbage. We don't have much in common, but we can at least amuse ourselves with a pack of cards. It must have been after eleven when we finally retired.'

'Had Bridget returned by then?'

'Good gracious, I couldn't tell you. She slept in Jason's room, you see, and would have entered by the door from the corridor. I can't remember hearing her come in, now that you ask me.'

'But the walls were thin enough for you to hear a sound from the nursery?'

'Oh, yes. There was a connecting door. I must have been asleep when she got back, the hussy, but I suppose a holiday is a holiday for the domestics too, if one looks at it from their point of view.'

'Now what about your husband, Ma'am?' said Cribb. 'What time did he return?'

'Prothero? God knows, darling. He was there in the morning and that's all I recollect. Have I helped you?'

'Substantially.'

She stood up. 'That's a weight off my mind, then. I'd hate to feel that I was hindering Scotland Yard in the execution of its duty. It's rather stuffy down here, don't you think? I wonder if it's safe to take a turn on the deck? If I could know for certain that Prothero is not on the pier—'

'I'll go and see,' volunteered Moscrop.

'You will? What a divinely generous man you are! Then if the sergeant escorts me—just on the seaward side for a few minutes—no one can think I've sold myself to perdition.'

The sight of Cribb's six foot one inch gallantly taking the air with Zena Prothero's five foot two was witnessed only by the seagulls, Moscrop very decently having mounted guard at the bulwarks on the port side.

'What do you think of him, darling?' she asked at once.

'Who, Ma'am?' He seemed to be addressing the top of her hat.

'Mr. Moscrop. Who else?'

'I'm not sure,' said Cribb, truthfully. 'What's your opinion?'

'Not to be relied upon, my dear. Harmless enough, I'm sure, but distinctly odd in his behaviour. I haven't said a word to Prothero, but he follows me around! You don't think I encourage him, darling, do you?'

'I'm sure you don't mean to, Ma'am, but he appears to have led a somewhat sheltered existence. I don't think he understands much about the ways of the ladies.'

'Lord, you're right! He regards us all as racehorses, things to be watched through field-glasses. I only asked him to take the sleeping preparation to the chemist to give him something useful to do.'

'You weren't worried about what you were taking, then?'

'Worried isn't the word, darling. Curious, perhaps. Yes, I was curious. Prothero isn't communicative, you see. It was a harmless errand to send the poor little man on. He must have been disappointed on Saturday night when Bridget came down to collect the chemist's report, poor lamb, but I had no choice, as I explained.'

Cribb stopped and put his hands on the side-rail. 'Well, if it achieved nothing else, Ma'am, at least you now know what your husband mixes for you. A dose of laudanum as mild as that wouldn't hurt a child, let alone a grown woman.'

She looked keenly at him. 'But, of course. Prothero is a doctor, darling. He knows about these things.'

They resumed their walk, Zena supporting her hat-brim as the breeze stiffened.

'I don't know whether you've read anything in the newspapers about the tragedy I'm in Brighton to investigate, Ma'am?'

'Very little, I must confess,' said Zena. '*The Morning Post* had only a small paragraph. I don't believe it mentioned your name, even.'

'It was the Brighton newspapers that gave the fullest accounts, quite naturally. You won't have read about the jacket that was dug up on the beach, then?'

'Jacket? I don't believe I did.'

'Black sealskin. A coat of good quality. Better than the other clothes we found. I heard that you owned such a jacket, Ma'am. Is that correct?'

'Why, yes. I do.'

Cribb nodded. 'You see how we connected the tragedy with you?'

'I suppose so,' Zena said. 'But dozens of women own sealskin jackets. They're fashionable, darling.'

'Not so many have a top button that's had to be sewn back on with different cotton. Yours has, I understand.'

She frowned. 'As a matter of fact, that is true. But I don't see—'

'And did you buy yours last spring at Fremantle's of Dorking?'

'My dear, I did, but what are you trying to prove?'

'That's where the jacket on the beach came from,' said Cribb grimly. 'Do you have yours at home, Ma'am?'

'I don't believe I do. I left it with some other things at the Albemarle. Prothero will bring it home on Saturday.'

'With respect, I don't think so.'

She stopped and looked up at him. 'What do you mean? Are you telling me that *my* coat—'

'Is the one we found? Yes, Ma'am. I'll get you to identify it later, of course, but I'm no longer in any doubt about it. The dead woman was wearing your sealskin jacket last Saturday night.'

Zena was shaking her head. 'It's quite impossible.'

Cribb took her arm. 'Not at all, my dear. You know as well as I do that it was your servant, Bridget, who was murdered.'

Silence, while she assimilated what Cribb had said.

'It's not unknown for a servant to borrow something from the family wardrobe,' he went on. 'Smart jacket. Fashionable, you say. Mistress asleep.'

'Who said I was asleep?' demanded Zena.

'It's the only explanation. Shall we look at what you've already told me? Jason was so fretful that you decided to go back to Dorking with him on Sunday, bringing your holiday to a premature end.'

'Absolutely true.'

'Pains in his stomach, you decided. Poor little fellow must have suffered something dreadful for you to abandon your husband like that. When did the crying start?'

'Heavens, I can't remember that.'

'It was bad on Saturday, though?'

'Yes, I haven't denied it.'

'Yet you tell me that you spent the evening watching fireworks and playing cards and that after Bridget had been down to get the formula from Mr. Moscrop you gave her the evening off.'

She coloured. 'The child was quieter by then.'

Cribb shook his head slowly. 'With rockets and Chinese crackers going off underneath his window? I can't believe that, Ma'am. It makes no sense and I'll not embarrass you any more by persisting with the point. I think Jason was asleep, as a matter of fact. Bridget had given him a dose of your sleeping-draught.'

'The laudanum!' Zena was wide-eyed with horror. 'She fed that to a tiny child!'

Cribb scratched the tip of his nose. 'I must confess that I misled you there, Ma'am. The sleeping-potion wasn't laudanum, as Mr. Moscrop will confirm. I needed to know if you had ever seen the chemist's analysis. It's obvious you hadn't. We found it on the beach, you see, near the sealskin jacket and the—er—other items. Bridget still had it with her, tucked up her sleeve, I dare say, or wherever ladies tuck such things. It's chloral you've been taking, if you're still interested. Relatively harmless. You took it as usual on Saturday, didn't you, leaving Bridget to deal with Mr. Moscrop? You didn't realise that when you were unconscious she'd come back from seeing Moscrop, borrow your jacket and probably give Jason a spoonful of chloral to assist his slumbers before going out to enjoy herself—as she thought. We know what happened to her.'

She lowered her eyelids. 'You must think me very foolish, Sergeant, to have attempted to deceive you.'

'Not foolish, Ma'am. I understand your reasons. If I may say so, it was a spirited account of the fireworks, considering you weren't awake at the time.'

She smiled faintly. 'One goes to extreme lengths to avoid a scandal when one's living is founded on public confidence, as ours is. The smallest suggestion of anything improper can decimate a medical practice, Sergeant. I'm sure you'll find Bridget's murderer and bring him to trial, but he can expect to receive more justice than we shall. There is no question that in the eyes of my husband's patients as they read their newspapers in Dorking we shall be condemned, without reference to a judge and jury. Who is going to consult a doctor whose name is mentioned in connection with a murder, whose wife is shown to be dependent upon a sleeping-drug and whose son swam on a public beach with a female servant? There is no question of it: we shall have to move away, hoping that when our names are no longer household words we can purchase a practice in some other part of the country. But I wonder whether we shall survive at all as a family. We have lived with secrets, Sergeant, things that will rend us apart when they are revealed, as now they must be. In my weakness I stood by while Guy indulged in his silly antics in the sea with Bridget, knowing it would cause the gravest offence to my husband, but believing he would never have cause to know about it.'

'Perhaps he guessed the truth,' said Cribb.

She shook her head. 'Never. He would have stopped it at once. I had my instructions, but I was not equal to them. Yet that is not all that I dread. When my husband went out by afternoon and evening, sometimes returning very late, I kept telling myself that I believed his stories of visiting former patients. For peace of mind I did not seek to discover the truth, Sergeant—how many thousand neglected women have done the same?—I took my sleeping preparation and sought oblivion. But now there will be no escape from the truth. I shall hear where he was on Saturday and I do not know what I shall have to forgive. I do not know whether the removal of our illusions is the best thing. Sergeant, is it so unforgivable to have tried in our clumsy way to conceal the fact that Bridget was probably your dead woman on the beach?'

'I'm in no position to forgive it, Ma'am,' said Cribb, 'but when you put it that way I can understand.'

14

'Now, THACKERAY. I'VE TOLD you about *my* meeting with Mrs. Prothero. I'd be obliged if you'd give me your account of the meeting you had with Miss Floyd-Whittingham.'

Thackeray took out his pocket-notebook and cleared his throat in the best police-court manner. He was now becoming accustomed to the solemn little exchanges of information in the interviewing-room at Grafton Street police station, but the first time it had happened you could have knocked him down with a police-issue pencil. It was contrary to everything he knew about Cribb's way of conducting inquiries. Anyone assisting Cribb was expected to glean a full understanding of developments from listening for occasional utterances never more than half a dozen words in length and watching for the tell-tale tilt of an eyebrow, or the twitch of a cheek-muscle. There were rumours, of course, that after Cribb's music hall murder investigation, criticism had been voiced in certain quarters of sergeants who ordered constables to perform manoeuvres in ignorance of their full implications, but Cribb was unlikely to be influenced by *that*. It was far more likely that the Brighton ozone had gone to his head.

'In accordance with my instructions,' Thackeray began, 'I proceeded to Lewes Crescent, arriving there shortly after eleven o'clock. Upon knocking at the door and announcing my business I was admitted by a maidservant who informed me that Miss Floyd-Whittingham was at breakfast. I impressed upon her the seriousness of my business and she agreed to take me to her Mistress without delay. I followed in anticipation of being admitted to the breakfast-room, but found myself instead being led upstairs and shown into what—er—not to beat about the bush—I found to be Miss Floyd-Whittingham's bedroom.'

'Her *bedroom?*' Cribb brought down his hand noisily on his thigh. 'Thackeray, how do you manage it? You can make a compromising situation out of anything. Where was Miss Samantha, then?'

'In bed, Sarge. With a boiled egg on a silver tray.' He resumed his evidence-giving manner. 'Naturally, I apologised for the intrusion, but she did not give the appearance of being discomfited.'

'She didn't disappear screaming under the bedclothes, you mean? Go on.'

'She was decently covered with a white lace garment. I sat on a chair—it was quite ten feet from the bed—and explained the reason for my visit. I handled it delicate, Sarge, as you suggested, saying we was tracing the movements of a number of people on Saturday night. She admitted quite readily that she was at the ball with Dr. Prothero—called him Gregory. They was in the Dome from nine o'clock onwards, except for half an hour when they watched the fireworks from the Steine Gardens. That was between half past nine and ten. Otherwise they was there until one in the morning. She's got a card with his name against the dances to prove it, Lancers and Galopades and Polkas. Gregory all the way down to the Last Waltz. She'll vouch for him, I'm sure.'

'Hm. Did she volunteer anything else about him—where she met him, for instance?'

'In church, Sarge. She didn't know he was married at first. He's always behaved very proper, she said. He's a decent, warm-hearted man and his wife don't understand him.'

Cribb gave the celebrated tilt of the right eyebrow. 'That's one view of Prothero, then. What about Samantha? What's your opinion of her, Constable?'

Thackeray tilted *both* eyebrows. 'Oh, a regular beauty, Sarge! No question of it. A face like a china doll and a show of red hair I've never seen the equal of. I suppose she wears it different when she goes out, but it was hanging loose down her back when I saw it. I don't know what she's like dressed and on her feet, Sarge, but she's a stunner in bed, I promise you!'

Cribb winced. 'I believe it Thackeray, but I wouldn't bandy it about in quite those terms if I were you. People jump to wrong conclusions.'

'What bothers me,' said Thackeray, undaunted, 'is what a handsome young woman like that sees in a man of Prothero's age—even allowing that he's a dapper little toff.'

'Oh, it's not so unusual,' said Cribb.

'You're right, Sarge! I do believe there's a type of young woman that finds older men difficult to resist. I observed a certain look in Miss Floyd-Whittingham's eyes as I entered the room.'

'Focused on a grey beard, perhaps?' murmured Cribb. 'It sounds as though you had a lucky escape, Thackeray. You *did* escape, I take it? Never mind. We've more important things to discuss. Between us, we've now interviewed everyone who would seem to be connected with this case—Miss Floyd-Whittingham, the Protheros and Mr. Moscrop. I suppose there's still the possibility of some complete stranger having met Bridget on the beach on Saturday night and murdered her, but in my experience that sort of killer doesn't go to a deal of trouble afterwards to get rid of the body. No, I think we've met our murderer already. You've got your notebook there, and I've seen you working at it on and off throughout the week. If it wasn't the Newmarket Handicap you were considering, I hope you've got something useful to contribute to the investigation by now.'

Thackeray was not unprepared. He licked his forefinger in a businesslike way and turned several pages of the notebook. 'Well, Sarge, you've always advised me to look for a motive in a murder case, and I've been weighing up the parties concerned to see what reason they would have for putting an end to Bridget.'

'A sound procedure, Constable. What conclusions have you reached?'

'Ah. Well, let's dismiss the least likely one first. So far as I can tell, Miss Floyd-Whittingham has never met Bridget, and wouldn't have any reason to kill her. The only way she might be involved is as an accomplice to Dr. Prothero.'

'Reasonable enough,' said Cribb. 'And she doesn't sound to me like the sort of woman who's handy with a cleaver.'

'Them's my own sentiments exactly, Sarge. And I've got the same reservations about Mrs. Prothero from what you told me of her. She's got a motive, though, in my opinion.'

'What's that?'

'She didn't like Bridget at all. She told Moscrop Prothero engaged the girl himself. If she'd had her way she would have dismissed her. Now seeing that she's so attached to young Jason, and Bridget was apt to go off swimming with Guy and leave the child in the charge of bathing-machine attendants, it don't seem impossible to me that Mrs. Prothero might have got desperate, knowing that her husband didn't take no interest. You told me yourself that Mrs. P. knew about the capers in the sea with Guy, so she must have known about Jason being left with strangers, too. That's enough to strike panic into a woman of her nervous susceptibilities.'

'I see the point,' said Cribb, 'but there's still the dismembering to account for. That's not a woman's work.'

Thackeray had obviously thought of this. He tucked his thumbs confidently in the pockets of his waistcoat and said, 'A woman as charming as Mrs. Prothero might not have to look very far to find a man prepared to wield a cleaver for her.'

'Moscrop?' said Cribb.

Thackeray rewarded his sergeant with a broad grin. 'But I'll leave him for a moment, if you don't mind. The next on the list is Guy.'

'The boy?'

'Now that's just it, Sarge. We're disposed to think of him as a boy, but he's fifteen years old and quite precocious from what I've heard. It ain't every fifteen-year-old that talks to his elders and betters the way that lad does, or takes snuff, or has a dabble below stairs, to use a coarse expression.'

'That doesn't make him a murderer.'

'Ah, but he ain't what you would call a level-headed personality. Perhaps it's on account of his age—I'm not sure about these things—but he sounds to me like a boy without a proper sense of responsibility. Moscrop says he saw him holding Jason above the crocodile tank. That's the deuce of a risk to take with a small child, wouldn't you say? He seems to have no respect for people at all, in his family or out of it. Now just suppose his philanderings with Bridget had gone a good deal further than the Protheros realised. Just suppose Bridget was in a delicate condition, or thought she was, at any rate, and told him so. I can't help wondering whether he ain't the sort of boy that might resort to murder in that situation.'

'It's plausible,' admitted Cribb.

'And so we come to Dr. Prothero,' Thackeray went on, like a guide in a museum, turning the page of his notebook. 'Now, here's an interesting thing, Sarge. Moscrop told us that when he had his conversation with Bridget on the morning of the regiment's march-past, it was she who gave him Miss Floyd-Whittingham's name. She knew all about the goings-on at Lewes Crescent of an afternoon. And that was at a time when Mrs. Prothero herself thought the doctor was going the rounds of his former patients. It's tailor-made for blackmail, in my opinion. I think that's why Bridget was able to keep her job, even when Mrs. Prothero knew she was neglecting Jason. Prothero wasn't going to dismiss her when he knew she could blow the gaff to his wife.'

'Do you think he was paying Bridget money, then?'

'That's hard to say. She may have been satisfied with keeping her job. In those circumstances drawing a wage is a kind of blackmail, in my estimation. Well, Sarge, that's the motive in Prothero's case. Bridget demands too much, so he kills her.'

'Leaving us with Mr. Albert Moscrop.'

'Yes. I've left him till last deliberate, Sarge, because I think he's the deepest one of the lot. It's not that I'm unappreciative of all the information he's given us. We wouldn't have got this far so quick without him.'

'You wonder why he's so interested in the case?'

'Well, you must admit that it's a curious way to spend a holiday. I've seen the jokes in *Punch* about men at the seaside peering through spy-glasses, but I've never come across anyone with a whole bagful of telescopes and binoculars. For all his grand ideas about being in Brighton for the season, he's got no intention of going to balls or parties. He just watches everyone else enjoying themselves.'

'Eccentric,' said Cribb, 'but harmless.'

'Ah, yes, up to a point, Sarge. But when the glasses settle on a married woman and won't move off, then I'm not so sure if it is harmless. Allowing for the sort of man he is, deadly serious but completely inexperienced with the fair sex, I'd say that any woman at the far end of those binoculars should watch out. It's the men of his age and his kind that get strange notions in their heads. They can very easily convince themselves that the unfortunate women they fix upon are encouraging 'em, and that can lead to ugly results.'

'It's an interesting idea,' said Cribb, 'except for the fact that it was Bridget who was murdered, and not Zena Prothero.'

'But don't you see,' said Thackeray, passionately, 'that a man with such a single-minded interest in a woman is going to be ruthless in pursuing her? I don't think that child Jason strayed away from his mother on the beach. I think Moscrop abducted him—just to bring him back to her and provide himself with a reason for talking to her. A man in that frame of mind will do *anything*, Sarge.'

'Hold on a bit!' said Cribb. 'Single-minded, I'll give you. Humourless, yes. Capable of contriving some situation to meet Mrs. Prothero, yes. But *anything!* That won't do, Constable. It's woolly. Not the way a detective should think. If there's a motive for Moscrop, there must be a clearly-reasoned argument, however odd the man may be.'

'I was coming to that, Sergeant,' protested Thackeray. 'You'll allow that he formed a strong attachment for Mrs. Prothero?'

'Yes.'

'So strong that he went to some trouble to find out for himself about her husband's unfaithfulness?'

'I should think that was his reason, yes.'

'And he felt protective towards Mrs. Prothero, and angry about the husband who didn't appreciate her?'

'Yes.'

'Well it seems to me that things was building up to a

crisis-point on the Saturday, the day of the murder. Mrs. Prothero had asked Moscrop to get the sleeping-potion analysed. By that time, he was ready to be her slave. He thought Dr. Prothero was contemptible. It was even possible—and I'm not putting it any stronger, Sarge—that the sleeping potion might contain some kind of slow-acting poison. Anyway, being asked to get it analysed was being put into a privileged position.'

'You're doing better now,' said Cribb.

'So Moscrop must have felt highly pleased with himself, meeting her in secret by the croquet-lawn and arranging another secret meeting for the Saturday, when he would give her the chemist's analysis. She was sure to be in a grateful frame of mind. It would be Saturday night in Brighton. The fireworks would be under way. She might even agree to take a walk along the prom. with him. Imagine the prospect of that to a man who had hardly talked to a woman outside his telescope-shop!'

'Careful, Thackeray,' warned Cribb. 'Let's leave imagination out of it.'

Thackeray returned a sharp glance. 'Well, the facts are,' he said with emphasis, 'that he chanced to meet Bridget in the Steine on Saturday morning and discovered that she knew all about him following her mistress and even the secret meetings. That was sure to be a severe shock to him. He was accustomed to being alone and watching other people from a secret, solitary position. Now he discovered that Bridget, this common servant-girl, knew a rare amount of what was going on. Then in the evening, when he went to meet his Zena, who should come instead, but Bridget! The formula never got back to Mrs. Prothero because Moscrop took Bridget along the beach and killed her. She must have become a nightmare to him and he found the quickest way he could of finishing it. Afterwards he hid the body in the arch and set about planning to dispose of it in his usual methodical way.'

'Admirable!' said Cribb, genuinely impressed. 'Can you explain why he told us so much about his doings, though? Wasn't it in his interest not to have anything to do with the police?'

'I don't think so, Sarge. He'd met Guy as well as Zena. They would have been sure to have mentioned his name when the questions began. It was clever thinking on his part to anticipate all that and volunteer to help us. Of course, he pretended to believe it was Zena whose body was found at first. That way he could seem to be just as surprised as anyone when it was found that Bridget was the victim. In short, Sergeant,' Thackeray ended triumphantly, 'I think we ought to run him in.'

'Wait a moment!' said Cribb. 'What about the others—Mrs. Prothero and her servant problem, Guy in prospect of being a papa and Dr. Prothero undergoing blackmail? Do we forget about them just because Moscrop had a strong motive?'

Thackeray frowned. 'But they couldn't possibly have done it. They all had alibis. Mrs. Prothero was drugged with chloral and asleep, Guy was in the hotel, watching the fireworks from the balcony, and the doctor was at the ball all evening, except for half an hour in Steine Gardens which he spent with Miss Floyd-Whittingham. If you want to be quite sure, we could see if Moscrop's got a criminal record. A man like that could very well have been in trouble before.'

Cribb opened the drawer of the desk in front of him and took out a sheet of paper. 'All right. How's this for a record? "August, 1881, Hove, criminal assault upon a minor, one Matthew Hawkins, not brought to court. December, 1881, Eastbourne, indecent assault upon a servant-girl of 17 years, Jane Brett, not brought to court. June, 1882, Eastbourne, attempted murder of Jane Brett by strangulation, not brought to court."'

'Really, Sarge?' said Thackeray. 'We've got him this time for sure, then. "Not brought to court", indeed! Makes you wonder what the local force was up to. We'd better get along to Montpelier Parade and clap the darbies on him quick before he adds to the list.'

'Montpelier Parade?'

'The address of Moscrop's lodgings,' pointed out Thackeray, not altogether suppressing his surprise at Cribb's obtuseness.

'Ah. Now that wouldn't do.'

'Why not, Sarge?'

'Because it ain't Moscrop's record. So far as I've been able to check, he's never put a foot wrong in his life. You couldn't really call this a record at all, come to that, could you? Three cases, none of 'em brought to court. I put it together myself, from information received, as they say. It's more of a school record than a criminal one, since all the information comes from headmasters. There's nothing like a small private school for hushing up a scandal, paying reparation to the victim and pushing the offender on to some other place of learning. Sometimes it's the masters that go, and sometimes the boys. Boy in this case.'

'Do you mean Guy?' Thackeray was open-mouthed.

Cribb nodded. 'Well, you had him on your list, so don't be too despondent.'

'But he had an alibi. He was in the hotel all evening with his mother. Moscrop saw him on the balcony.'

'His mother was asleep, if you remember. Once we established that, Guy had no alibi. The game of cribbage had to be pure invention. Oh, yes, he was seen on the balcony, but it was while Bridget was with Moscrop. After that, she went back to the hotel suite and out with Guy to see the fireworks, having borrowed Mrs. Prothero's jacket to add a little spice to the escapade.'

'But there's nothing to suggest she went back to the Albemarle, Sarge. She still had the chemist's report with her when she died.'

'Do you think she would have left it lying about up there? Her Mistress was out to the world until next morning. There was only Prothero himself to see it if she left it in the bedroom. She didn't want that so she took it with her. Besides, she *must* have gone back to put on the sealskin jacket. She wasn't wearing it when she met Moscrop.'

'He didn't say so, it's true, but—'

'He wouldn't have come to us suggesting Zena Prothero was dead if he'd seen Bridget wearing the jacket that night, now would he? He's an observant man, Constable.'

There was an interval while Thackeray rearranged his thoughts.

'When did you discover all this, Sarge?'

'About Guy? On the day I went to Dorking. I missed Zena Prothero, unfortunately, but I was able to get the names of

Guy's schools from the servants. The local police extracted the information I wanted from the headmasters at Hove and Eastbourne. There's quite a history of violence—torturing pet animals, bullying younger children and so on, leading up to a vicious attack on the boy Hawkins at Hove, but Guy is now of an age when he's turning his attention to women. The girl Jane Brett is fortunate to be alive. If there's such a thing as a born killer I would stake my reputation that Guy Prothero is it.'

'A madman, Sarge?'

'Sane in most respects, but with a lust for violence that makes him uncontrollable in certain situations.'

'His parents must have been at their wits' end when they got those reports from the schools,' said Thackeray.

'Prothero was inclined to disbelieve them, thinking the schools were exaggerating, until the attack on Jane Brett at Eastbourne. He was asked to take the boy away from school at once, and the headmaster urged his committal to an institution for the mentally deranged. As a medical man, Prothero was bound to consider the suggestion, unpalatable as it must have been. I don't believe he told his wife about the nature of the boy's outbursts at school—the "unspeakable thing" she mentioned to Moscrop was the disgrace of a second expulsion from school. If she'd known that Guy had attacked a servant-girl she certainly wouldn't have countenanced his going off to swim with Bridget.'

'Yet Prothero himself was quite agreeable to Guy swimming with the girl. You told me that yourself, Sarge. "A bit of spooning under the waves," he called it.'

Cribb nodded. 'That was his attitude *after* Bridget's death.

He knew his son to be a murderer by then. By posturing as a "forward thinker" he was trying to remove suspicion from Guy. It became clear that he'd changed his attitude when I interviewed Mrs. Prothero. She was thoroughly alarmed at the prospect of his finding out about the bathing with Bridget. "He would have stopped it at once," she said. "I had my instructions, but I was not equal to them." Prothero had strictly forbidden any such thing. He knew what the consequences might be. Afterwards it was smarter to suggest that he knew exactly what was going on and didn't disapprove.'

'He was protecting the boy all along, then?'

'Protecting his own reputation too. Yes, he lied, of course, when he told me that his wife had returned to Dorking with Jason and Bridget. I repeated the question to be quite sure about it.'

'Was that what first made you suspect Guy, Sarge?'

'Well, it was obvious enough that the Protheros were lying. Their stories were full of inconsistencies. I suppose they hadn't had time to think the thing out and rehearse what they were going to say. There was one point when Prothero was ready to say that his wife was asleep on the night of the murder and Guy was trying to convince me she was awake. There wasn't the trust between the members of the family that a strong united alibi demands. They were all suspicious of each other in their various ways. Prothero was determined not to let Guy know what he was planning for *him* when the holiday was over.'

'An asylum, Sarge?'

'Something of the sort, I suspect. But Zena Prothero knew nothing of this. I'm convinced that the doctor regarded the boy as his responsibility—he wasn't Zena's child, after all—and was determined that she should not become involved. Possibly Guy confessed to him, or he caught the boy coming home in the small hours. At any rate, Prothero knew by Sunday morning that Guy had murdered Bridget. He arranged at once for Zena to return to Dorking—probably dosed Jason with something to make him feverish—telling her that Bridget was unaccountably missing. Later she must have read in the newspaper about the human remains found on the beach, and the sealskin jacket. She believed—and still believes—that Bridget went out that night wearing her jacket and was killed by some stranger. She telegraphed Prothero from Dorking saying she must meet him urgently at the Devil's Dyke. She wanted to tell him what she feared, you see. He met her, listened to her story, and gave her the knapsack containing some of Bridget's clothes to carry away, impressing upon her that if it were known that *their* servant had been murdered, the Dorking practice would be in ruins. The Worthing police picked up the knapsack this morning. It contained a pair of shoes, stays, stockings, a camisole and a bonnet—the missing clothes Bridget was wearing when she was murdered, complete with fish-scales adhering to 'em.'

'From the arch where the body was dismembered? Did Prothero do that, do you think?'

'Difficult to say. It didn't look like a doctor's handiwork, but then Prothero ain't fool enough to give himself away like that. I'm inclined to think he must have supervised the disposing of the body. We're examining their clothes for bloodstains, of course.'

Thackeray started in surprise. 'Do you mean that you've got their clothes already, Sarge? Is the boy in custody?'

'The answer to your first question is yes. To your second, no. Guy and his father left Brighton this morning on horseback. It's all right, Constable! No panic! The police all the way from here to Dorking have been alerted and there's a plain-clothes man following them. They left a trunk at the Albemarle to be called for, and Inspector Pink and his men have very obligingly picked it up. It surprises me that Prothero stayed so long in Brighton. It was two weeks yesterday that Bridget was killed. It's a cool customer that can sit it out as long as that when an investigation's afoot. Ah!'

The interruption was from P.C. Thomas, bearing a telegram.

'As I expected,' said Cribb. 'They stopped at Horsham for lunch. *The Fortune of War.* I suggest that we—Good God!' He put the telegram down and pressed his hand to his forehead.

'What is it, Sarge? What on earth's the matter?'

'The matter is, Constable,' said Cribb in a strange voice, 'that I've made a fatal error of judgement. According to this telegram, our suspect died shortly after one o'clock.'

'*Died?*' repeated Thackeray. 'It must be a mistake, Sarge. They mean "dined".'

'I'd believe you,' said Cribb, 'if it didn't go on to ask for my instructions regarding the post mortem.'

CHAPTER 15

THE DRIVE TO HORSHAM by police-van was distinguished by a total absence of conversation, Cribb hunched in the corner seat, eyes fixed on the window but seeing nothing of the passing countryside, Thackeray busying himself wiping his forehead with his handkerchief, straightening his necktie and retying his boot-laces. After a little over an hour the driver reined outside *The Fortune of War*, a small hotel on the Guildford Road, some three-quarters of a mile beyond the town. Cribb's brown study came to a decisive end. 'Come, Thackeray! We're late enough on the scene as it is.'

The constable on duty in the foyer, not having seen the police-van's arrival, raised a cautionary hand, which snaked resourcefully into a salute as Thackeray muttered, 'The Yard,' and Cribb stalked past. Ahead, a white card was suspended from the door-knob of one of the two lounges. It announced with apologies that patrons were temporarily requested to refrain from using the room. Cribb advanced on the door as if this were an invitation, opened it, and found a police inspector, a manifestly disconcerted hotel manager and Dr. Prothero.

'Scotland Yard?' echoed the inspector, after Cribb had explained who he was. 'It was you that asked us to have men available, then. A notable feat of anticipation, Sergeant. I only wish that you had warned us to expect something as sanguinary as this. Had we known—'

'Had *I* known, I'd have prevented the boy from leaving Brighton,' said Cribb. 'You've established the circumstances surrounding his death, I expect, sir?'

'I have indeed. The facts are these, Sergeant. This gentleman, Dr. Prothero, and his son arrived here at about ten minutes after twelve o'clock and arranged for their horses to be watered. They then ordered lunch and had glasses of sherry in the ante-room while it was being prepared. At a quarter to one they took their places in the dining-room, which was otherwise empty. They were served the following—and I shall now refer to my notebook, because the details may well be important—tomato soup, followed by roast beef, with roast potatoes, buttered parsnips, Brussels sprouts, Yorkshire pudding, gravy and horse-radish sauce, followed by apple charlotte with cream, followed by coffee. It was some twenty minutes after the coffee was served that the boy displayed symptoms of unease—not indigestion, as one might suppose after a substantial meal, but shortness of breath. This seemed at first to be the consequence of an over-enthusiastic inhalation of snuff, but it soon became apparent that something much worse was the matter. Within ten minutes he was dead. There was nothing that Dr. Prothero or Mr. Wood, here, the manager, could do to save him. The doctor, I think, can best describe the nature of the collapse—if that is not too distressing, sir.'

Certainly the strain of a severe shock showed in Prothero's face. He looked at no one, and addressed his account of his son's death to the back of his hand, which he turned in several positions as he was talking, as if it held some clue to the tragedy. 'Guy died of an acute attack of asthma. The onset was very sudden: a short period of restlessness, then accelerated breathing accompanied by coughing and retching. We supported him and loosened his clothing and endeavoured to calm him, but the respiration became progressively slower and more laboured, with severe broncho-spasms. Within minutes there were several convulsions and he stopped breathing.'

There was a pause before Cribb asked, 'Were the first symptoms you described consistent with other attacks of asthma Guy had experienced?'

Prothero replied in the same automatic way, without a glance in Cribb's direction. 'Generally similar, yes. There had been nothing so severe before. On previous occasions I have injected atropine to prevent constriction of the bronchioles, but on this occasion I had none of my equipment with me.'

'How do you account for so sudden an attack?'

'There *is* no accounting for asthma,' said Prothero. 'We in the profession are only too conscious of the limitations in our knowledge. A hundred different things might have provoked the attack. The most negligible, intangible things—animal emanations, for example. The late Dr. Hyde Salter, the author of the standard work on the subject, was himself asthmatic and established a definite relationship between his own asthma and the presence of a cat.'

'Our cats are never allowed in the lounges,' protested the manager at once.

'That was merely an example,' said Prothero wearily. 'There may be a hundred other agents of the complaint. Pollen, for instance, is known to induce hay-fever.'

The inspector looked up with the suddenness indicative of an inspiration. 'Do you think that the horses—'

'He has ridden horses since he was a small child,' said Prothero, 'and never suffered a reaction. Nor is there likely to be any connection with the meal which you have recorded so slavishly in your pocket-book. Asthma is a respiratory disorder, not a digestive one.'

'Are you quite sure, Doctor, that your son's death was due to asthma?' asked Cribb.

'Haven't I indicated that already? I know what I am talking about, Sergeant. I have written a dozen monographs on the subject. Examine the boy's body and you will find the classic indications of asthmatic death: the slightly bluish tinge to the colouring, the clammy feel of the skin arising from the heavy perspiration and the quick drop in temperature, and the characteristic clenching of the hands.'

Cribb went to the ottoman, lifted the sheet that had been draped over Guy's body and verified everything Prothero had said.

'I shall therefore make out a death certificate indicating that he died from natural causes,' said Prothero.

'And I shall ask the coroner for authority for a post mortem examination,' said Cribb. 'The circumstances warrant it, sir, as I'm sure you'll appreciate. And in the meantime I shall be obliged if you will advise me of all your movements so that I may keep in touch with you.'

'I propose to return to Dorking,' said Prothero, 'and I shall be there until further notice.' And he added in a lower tone, 'With your permission, of course, Sergeant Cribb.'

After Prothero had left the room, with the manager in tow, probably mindful of the unpaid bill, the inspector asked Cribb, 'What do you expect to get from a post mortem? It's a clear case of asthma.'

'Looks like that, sir.'

'Surely you don't expect to prove that it was induced in some way? You'd never convince a jury of that, Sergeant.'

'No, sir.'

'Well in that case I'm damned if I can see the point of going to the trouble of a post mortem examination.'

'That's where we differ, then, sir. I suppose I see it from another point of view. Today I was ready to arrest Guy Prothero for the Brighton beach murder. The boy was a homicidal maniac. I should have arrested him a week ago if I hadn't had to grope my way through a welter of false statements invented by his family. Quite apart from any protective sentiments the Protheros had towards him, their own livelihood was at stake, you see. Respectable general practice in a country town—imagine the effect of a sensational murder trial on that. Now in my experience people of their station in life generally have a way of dealing with the member of the family who threatens to create a scandal; there's private institutions that cater for almost any human aberration you can think of if someone's prepared to pay. Guy Prothero would probably have been committed to some asylum for the well-to-do if he hadn't gone as far as murder. That altered things. When it gets as serious as that, the law can't be bought off, you see. Justice has to run its course. Oh, they wriggled and squirmed and tried to avoid it, but I was closing in day by day. And, as I tell you, I was ready to make the arrest today. What happens? The boy suffers a fatal attack of asthma on the way home. If that sounds like pure chance to you, sir, you're entitled to believe it. If you tell me asthmatic death can't be induced, I'll take your word for it, but that won't stop me from using every means at my disposal to ascertain whether it *was* asthma that killed Guy Prothero.'

Inspector Wood frowned. 'You'll find it difficult to get round those symptoms, Sergeant. The manager was there as a witness. I questioned him closely before I interviewed Dr. Prothero. He described it all in a layman's terms, of course, but his statement bears out everything you heard the doctor say. It's a singular thing to have happened, as you imply, but I think we have to reconcile ourselves to the fact that the boy died from natural causes.'

As if not one word of the inspector's had percolated into his thoughts, Cribb asked, 'What happened to the plates they ate from?'

'Fortunately they hadn't been washed when I arrived,' said the inspector. 'I had them put aside with the sherry glasses and the coffee cups as a matter of routine. One never knows, in cases of sudden death.'

'Good,' said Cribb, the gleam at last returning to his eye.

'I'd like everything analysed by the best man available. As a matter of routine, sir,' he added. 'One never knows.'

Over a pint of half and half that evening, when all the arrangements had been made and every possible scrap of evidence removed to be examined by experts, Thackeray was sufficiently encouraged by Cribb's more buoyant mood to observe, 'You've worked out how Prothero could have arranged it, haven't you, Sarge? It's something the boy was given to eat or drink, something that could bring on an attack like that.'

Cribb gazed contemplatively into the beer-glass. 'Just an idea, Thackeray. A memory of something I read. D'you remember the Wimbledon poisoning case last spring?'

'That doctor?'

'Yes. Lamson. Hanged at Wandsworth Prison for murdering his young brother-in-law. It interested me at the time because of the poison he employed—none of your conventional arsenic or strychnine. No, it was a doctor's choice of poison, so rarely used that the lawyers could find only one other case to quote during the trial, and again the poisoner was a doctor. Aconitine, Thackeray. People grow it in their gardens and call it wolf's-bane. The leaf is not unlike parsley, and the roots, if I remember correct, bear a close resemblance to horse-radish.'

'Horse-radish! Blimey, Sarge! Horse-radish sauce!'

'But let's not leap to conclusions, Constable. Lamson's victim took nearly four hours to die. Guy was dead within an hour of eating his lunch.'

'A strong dose, Sarge?'

'I don't know,' said Cribb. 'We'll need to find out more about it from the experts. The symptoms, so far as I recall, begin a few minutes after the poison is taken—a numbing of the mouth and throat, obstructing the victim's breathing. Stomach pains, vomiting and convulsions. Breathing becomes progressively feebler, and eventually death is due to asphyxia or shock. Close enough to Guy's symptoms to make it worth investigating, anyway.'

'Worth investigating, Sarge? I should think you've got it! He finally decided that he couldn't save his son from the gallows, so he saved his own reputation instead by slipping him the aconitine, knowing everyone would think it was asthma the boy had died of. It's a good thing you was there today or there wouldn't have been no post mortem at all!'

Cribb accepted this heart-felt tribute with a small shrug and added deprecatingly, 'The pity of it is that there's no chemical test for identifying aconitine in the human body. It's about the most difficult of all poisons to base a prosecution on. There are just two ways of identifying it: by taste and by administering it to animals. It's going to take more than a few dead mice to build a case against Prothero.'

'Could we find out if he purchased any of the stuff, Sarge?'

'That wouldn't help overmuch. A doctor might be expected to have some. It's recommended as an ointment for use in rheumatism and neuralgia.'

'Good Lord!' said Thackeray, his hand going rapidly to the small of his back.

'I'd stick to red flannel, if I were you,' said Cribb. 'Well, Constable. It's time we made our way back to Brighton, unless you fancy one for the road. The sherry of the house has quite a kick, I understand.'

'Takes your breath away,' said Thackeray, grinning widely.

■ But there were no grins at Scotland Yard later in the week when Thackeray found Cribb reading the post mortem report. 'I can't understand it,' the sergeant said at intervals, as his eyes travelled over the several sheets of finely-written hand-writing. At last he swept the report aside. 'Not a trace, Constable. Not aconitine, nor any other poison known to science. Nothing in the food, the drink or the contents of the stomach. They carried out the most exhaustive tests, injected frogs and mice with extracts, tried the effects of all the substances on the tongue and produced not one positive result. It's unbelievable.'

'You said it would be difficult to identify the poison, Sarge.'

'Yes, but a man was convicted last March on the evidence of less than a twentieth of a grain and our theory was that Guy was given a heavier dose. They were *looking* for it, Thackeray. Two of the leading pathologists in the land have signed that report.'

'Well, what *did* they report as the cause of death, Sarge?'

'Respiratory failure. The lungs were found to be uncommonly inflated. Constriction of the bronchial muscles, you see. Some retention of fluid in the lungs. Small haemorrhages on the underside of the diaphragm and in the viscera. I've read my medical books in the last few days, Constable. There's nothing there that ain't consistent with death from asthma.'

'It looks as though we're beaten, then.'

'Beaten?' said Cribb. 'We're on our own, Constable. That's the situation. We've got to think again. Get down the file with all the statements we took at Brighton. We'll start from the beginning again. We might never get Prothero into court, but I'm damned if I'll leave this case until I know how he did it.'

CHAPTER 16

ALBERT MOSCROP HAD BEEN back in London almost a week when Sergeant Cribb and Constable Thackeray called at the shop. For a moment he failed to recognise them; in his mind they were so firmly connected with his recent short vacation in Brighton that it was as preposterous as if the bathing-machine woman or the bicycle-boy had appeared in Oxford Street. Quite understandably he looked up from a lens he was polishing and simply saw two gentlemen customers. In his professional way he was deciding from their manner and appearance which counter was most appropriate to greet them from, the sporting or the astronomical, when Cribb's brisk salutation jolted him into realisation.

'Ah, Mr. Moscrop. Good to see you.'

He nodded vigorously. 'You too, Sergeant. And the constable, of course.'

'Smart shop,' said Cribb. 'Carpeted, too.'

'Thank you. Did you—er—'

'—wish to see you in private? If you please,' said Cribb.

They passed through a baize door into the rear of the shop. Instruments of every description were ranged about the small room. They had to move a large brass telescope before there was room to sit down on three stools.

'A most unexpected pleasure, Sergeant.'

'What was that?' said Cribb. 'Oh, our visit. Strictly business, Mr. Moscrop, strictly business. Possibly you heard of the—er—decease of young Guy Prothero.'

'At Horsham. Yes, I had got to hear of it. What a beastly tragedy for the family! An attack of asthma was responsible, I understand.'

'So we're told, sir, so we're told.'

'The boy was certainly a sufferer from periodic attacks of asthma. His mother told me so. I think that was why they tolerated his unsociable behaviour. I am sure that they were most solicitous about his health. He did disobey his father and indulge in secret bathing, of course, which might have upset him in some way, but there is a school of thought which says that nothing but good can come from sea-bathing. Now that I am back in London, I rather regret not having swum from the beach myself. I did take the plunge at Brill's, as I believe I told you.'

'You did, sir. There was something else you told me, another thing that Mrs. Prothero mentioned to you, I believe, and I want to ask you once again if you're quite sure about it.'

'Certainly, Sergeant. It must be something important if you have come here to verify it.'

'Could be very important, sir. When you made your

first statement in Brighton you told me the period of time the Protheros were proposing to spend there. D'you remember, sir?'

'Indeed I do. Zena told me when we first met. She said they had escaped from the practice at Dorking for three weeks. I distinctly remember remarking that I was planning to stay for the same length of time. Our holidays did not quite coincide, however, as they had already spent a week in Brighton before I arrived.'

'Three weeks,' said Cribb. 'Yet the doctor and the boy stayed for four.'

'Come to think of it, they must have. They were still in Brighton during my third week. What a singular thing. Perhaps the tragic passing of their servant delayed them. There are things one is obliged to attend to on occasions like that.'

Cribb shook his head. 'Everything could have been settled in a week, yet they stayed for fifteen days after Bridget's death. My investigation was going on all the while. Seems unlikely they were having such a jolly time that they couldn't bear to leave.'

'A week would represent a sizeable sacrifice of income for a doctor in practice,' said Moscrop.

'Good point. And so far as we know, the locum was standing in for three weeks, not four. But for some reason the doctor and his son extended their holiday by another week. When they did leave, it was a full *two* weeks after Mrs. Prothero and Jason. Important things must have kept them in Brighton.'

'But, Sergeant, I was observing Dr. Prothero almost without interruption. His daily routine continued unchanged, except for the day when he met his wife at the Dyke. The fourth week was a repetition of the others. There was no social function that he attended and the only appointments he had were with Miss Floyd-Whittingham.'

'*She* wasn't his reason for staying,' said Cribb, more to himself than Moscrop. 'He had more important things on his mind—principally Guy. The boy was liable to be arrested any time. Yet they stayed for another week, and Prothero did nothing and saw no one except his lady-friend. That's hard to account for. Then, at the end of the week, the boy conveniently died. Not at Dorking, you notice; that would open all sorts of sinister possibilities. At a hotel they'd never visited before, in the presence of an independent witness. "Asthma" on the death certificate and Dr. Prothero's problems were neatly solved. The question I have to answer—if I choose to feel suspicious, that is—is why it didn't happen a week before. And I think I'll take my question to Harley Street.'

Thackeray jerked up from his notes. 'Harley Street, Sarge?'

'That's our next call, Thackeray. I've made an appointment with one of London's foremost specialists in asthma. We're grateful for your help, Mr. Moscrop. If ever the Yard decides to equip its officers with telescopes, I'll put a word in, depend upon it.'

His mind reeling with the implications of what Cribb had said, Moscrop escorted the detectives through the shop to their cab.

■ The inquest on the late Guy Prothero the following week established that he died from natural causes. The medical evidence, the coroner pointed out, could lead to no other conclusion than that the boy was the victim of a chronic attack of asthma.

'You wouldn't object if I walked with you to the station?' said Cribb to Dr. Prothero, as they came down the court steps together. 'I presume you're going back to Dorking.'

'I am, as it happens,' said Prothero, without much warmth. 'By all means let us go that way together.' He set off at a rate suggesting he had no intention of prolonging the conversation.

'I'll be getting the same train,' said Cribb airily. 'I go to London, though. The next one should be the 4.23 if Bradshaw can be relied upon.'

Prothero put his hand to his watch-chain, but Cribb added, 'There's no need to check. There's a jeweller's opposite with a clock outside. D'you see? We've three-quarters of an hour in hand. Time for a good yarn, eh, Doctor?'

The prospect seemed to have a discouraging effect on Prothero, so Cribb went on, 'You'll be satisfied with the verdict, I dare say. It quite upheld your own opinion. Disposed of any doubts entertained by certain persons, eh? I should have known better than to question the opinion of a recognised authority, but, there, I'm trained to be a sceptic. Now that I've read your papers on the subject, I'm somewhat better informed.'

'You have read my monographs?' said Prothero, in surprise.

'Every one, Doctor. There's a very good library at the Royal College of Physicians. I ain't a member, but the Yard has certain connections with the profession, you know, and I can usually obtain what I want by mentioning a word in the right quarter. You make a regular splash in the index, having written so much. No trouble at all finding your writings. Very readable they are, too.'

'Thank you, but I had no idea—'

'That I was so interested? Insatiable curiosity, Doctor. It's a kind of habit. If I meet a man I like to know all about him. Not that I was reading your papers only, you understand. I had nearly a week in that library. Shall we cross? Devil of a lot of traffic. Market day, would you say?'

'Medicine must interest you,' Prothero observed, when they had safely negotiated the road.

'I find it irresistible,' said Cribb. 'When there's a problem to solve, that is. Take the case of your son's unfortunate death, for instance. Now the inquest's over and everything's settled, you might be surprised I should ever have harboured any uncertainty about the circumstances of his—er—going.'

'Oh, I can understand that any sudden death must be accounted for,' said Prothero, generously.

'We know that he murdered your servant Bridget,' Cribb said, as if he were talking about the weather. 'Probably strangled her, although we never found enough of her to tell for certain. It was strangling that nearly killed Jane Brett, the servant girl at the Eastbourne school, wasn't it? It must have been a regular nightmare to you and your wife. No wonder your memory of things was a little awry—when you said that Bridget went back to Dorking with your wife on the morning after the murder, for example. No, don't look alarmed, Doctor. If I were leading up to anything incriminating, I'd have a man with me and a pair of handcuffs in my pocket. It's your son I should have charged, and I left it too damned late. I've more important things to do than go over evidence looking for false statements. In a way, the boy's death closed the account for me. No further danger to the public, you see. I say, that looks a fetching plate of doughnuts. D'you fancy a pot of afternoon tea? We've time, you know. There's the station, not fifty yards away.'

Prothero acquiesced and presently found himself incarcerated in a bow-fronted tea-shop, watching Sergeant Cribb devour doughnuts as if he had not eaten for a week. Possibly the facilities at the Royal College had not included lunch.

'What was the object of your researches?' the doctor asked, steering the conversation in a more general direction.

Cribb bolted the rest of his third doughnut, raising a finger meanwhile to indicate the imminence of a response. 'I'm glad you asked me that. They were quite misdirected. I'm a stubborn cove, Doctor. Should have sought the advice of some authority such as yourself. Would have saved me several days' hard work. You see, I had it in my mind that Guy's death was—er—induced. It was just too neat to be believable. Record of asthma, inherited from his mother. Sudden attack, following a stiff ride on a horse and a heavy meal, both known to affect asthmatics. Symptoms observed by an independent witness. Post mortem evidence irrefutable.'

'How *could* the boy's death have been induced?' said Prothero. 'It is possible, I suppose, to arrange certain conditions which might bring on an attack of asthma, but it is most unlikely to result in death. If a patient were chronically ill anyway, I suppose it is not impossible to hasten his departure in such a way, but I have never heard of it. And Guy was quite a fit young man. Besides, this all happened in a public hotel. There *were* no irregular conditions. As for the horse-ride and the heavy meal, they were in no way unusual for Guy, as his headmasters, whom you appear to have been in touch with, will verify.'

'More tea?' said Cribb. 'I will, I think. What you must remember, Doctor, is that I'm a layman, knowing very little about asthma and its causes.'

'None of us knows very much.'

'After three days with the medical books and several consultations in Harley Street,' said Cribb, 'I came to that conclusion myself—and I was no further on with my theory. I had to look for something else. The devil of it was that everything was settled to everyone's satisfaction except mine. I'd thought it possible at one time that poison had been introduced, but the post mortem disposed of that explanation. There wasn't even a mark on the body to suggest foul play. So I decided to read through all my notes and statements again, hoping something would emerge. Two things did. The first was a remark your son himself made when the three of us were taking lunch at Mutton's, after my regrettable confusion over the bath-towel in Brill's Baths. He made a sort of outburst, you remember, accusing you of treating him no better than his half-brother, young Jason.'

'Certainly I remember. He was being deliberately provocative. I would not place too much reliance on anything he said if I were you, Sergeant.'

'One of his complaints was about a bruise on his arm from an injection. The size of half a crown, I think he said. You don't deny giving him one, Doctor?'

Prothero shook his head. 'I've no reason to deny it. I

injected a small quantity of atropine to relieve his asthma symptoms. It is a recognised way of preventing constriction of the bronchioles by inhibiting the action of the nervous system. Used by a physician, it is perfectly safe.'

'So I understand, sir,' said Cribb. 'It's a pity you had none with you on the day the boy died. An injection then might have saved him. But, of course, you weren't to know. Tell me, was it on the Sunday before we met at Brill's that you gave Guy his injection? That's what I've got in my notes.'

'Sunday? Yes, it would have been.'

'That's what the boy said. I can understand that he must have been in somewhat of a state that morning, with Bridget lying dead under the promenade, and your wife and second son being sent off double-quick to Dorking. I don't believe Mrs. Prothero knew what had happened, but I'm quite sure you did. A very anxious time for Guy, and most considerate of you to give him an injection, even if he *was* ungrateful later in the week when I met him. I suppose you must have been in quite a wax yourself on that Sunday morning, knowing what the boy had done and wondering what to do about it. Not at all surprising that the injection should have left a bruise. Was your hand shaking, Doctor?'

'I have no recollection,' said Prothero.

'I didn't expect you to have, sir, particularly as there was no sign of the mark fourteen days after, when the boy's body was examined. These things heal quickly, especially in the young. You don't mind if I have the last doughnut? It's more than I could do to leave it.'

'What was the other thing that emerged from the statements?'

Cribb chewed heartily and used the uneaten portion of the doughnut to emphasise his points. 'Ah, yes. The length of your holiday. Your wife said you were there for three weeks, but you stayed for four.'

'There were things to attend to, consequent upon the death of Bridget.'

Cribb smiled. 'I can well imagine, Doctor. But once the severed hand was discovered in the aquarium, on the Monday, there wasn't much prospect of disposing of the body, which was already dismembered. Just time, perhaps, to bury the head somewhere else in hope of preventing identification. But by the middle of the week the rest of the parcels were found. If you'd left the town at once, suspicions might have been aroused, I agree, but you could have left quite openly at the end of the week, when your holiday was due to finish. Instead, you *extended* it by a week.'

'It was only right that I should see things through, as Bridget's employer.'

Cribb dismissed this with a quick shake of the head. 'It *was* obvious to anyone that the matter had passed out of your control. Bridget was the subject of a murder inquiry, and an inquest was certain to be arranged. You could have been waiting for months if that was why you were still in Brighton. No, I think your motive was another one. You stayed there because of Guy, not Bridget. You *knew* he was going to die on the second Sunday after the murder. It was quite contrary to your plans that he should die at home in Dorking. There would have been no end of questions and suspicions. Instead, he died on the way home, in a public hotel, as you so rightly said.'

'I am supposed to have known all this? How do you imagine I possessed such clairvoyance, Sergeant?'

Cribb wiped his fingers with the table-napkin. 'No clairvoyance to it, sir. Timing, that's all. Fourteen days from the injection, Sunday to Sunday.'

'This is too preposterous!' said Prothero. 'Am I seriously supposed to have killed my own son with an injection of atropine that took effect two weeks after it was given, caused a violent death with all the symptoms of asthma and left no trace in the body? You had better spend some more time with the medical books, Sergeant. You have a lot to learn.'

'I appreciate that, Doctor. So when I formed my suspicions, I went back to the library to read all that I could find on the subject of injections—and the deuce of a lot there is. What caught my interest in particular were the inoculation experiments being carried out by Dr. Pasteur and others. In fact, it seems that half the doctors in Europe are busy pumping germs into dogs and guinea-pigs and publishing their results.'

Dr. Prothero sighed in a long-suffering way. 'Perhaps what you fail to appreciate, Sergeant, is that such experiments are intended to give protection against disease, in the same way as vaccination. Now that the organism responsible for typhoid fever has been discovered in Germany, for example, it is possible that we shall soon be able to inoculate the populace and so limit the spread of the disease. Experiments are already being conducted to that end.'

'So I read, sir. But it isn't quite so straightforward, is it? There are problems. While I was reading of these experiments I several times came across something the doctors describe as "acute respiratory shock", which seemed to have nothing at all to do with the disease under investigation. An animal that had been injected would suddenly appear to suffer extreme difficulty in breathing, followed by convulsions which frequently ended in death. Now this interested me a lot, so I went back to Harley Street to see if someone could explain a little more about it in simple terms comprehensible to a member of the Force, such as myself.'

'It is a phenomenon well known among doctors,' said Prothero.

'So I learned, sir, so I learned. But not so well known to the public. The medical profession is at pains not to reveal too much about it, since it only arises in connection with inoculation experiments. I have it on authority that a number of human patients are reported to have died in that way after experiments in Germany. It's liable to hold up mass-inoculation by several years until it's properly understood. But even if the doctors can't explain *why* it happens, they understand the conditions that are conducive to it.'

'The vaccines used in the German experiments were prepared with chick embryos, and the patients who died were sensitive to eggs. I don't know where this is leading us, Sergeant.'

'Don't you, sir? Well, as I understand it, the kind of violent reaction the doctors call acute respiratory shock can be induced in the laboratory. It was done as early as 1839 by the famous French physiologist, Francois Magendie, injecting dogs with egg-white. He discovered that two injections of egg-white at an interval of fourteen days produced acute respiratory shock. After the second injection the dogs died within five minutes. Now the curious thing is that egg-white isn't what you'd call a death-dealing substance. In fact, it's usually regarded as an antidote. It was obviously something to do with the period between the injections, because dogs injected after one week suffered no effect at all. More recently, a series of experiments on guinea-pigs produced the same dramatic result when they received a second injection of dog-serum.'

'You *have* been busy, Sergeant.'

'So the German doctors now believe that the acute respiratory shock in their patients was a similar reaction. The patients who died reacted to the vaccine, as you suggest, but some two weeks before receiving the injection they had become sensitised—is that the word?—to eggs, perhaps by eating them in some form, possibly even in a cake. When they were injected with the vaccine a fortnight later, the effect was as sudden and violent as if they had been given strychnine—except, of course, that the post mortem examination showed only the kinds of symptoms associated with death from chronic asthma.'

'Oh, it's eggs, is it?' said Prothero. 'I murdered my son with a boiled egg, did I—or was it a Madeira cake?'

'If you'll kindly allow me to go on,' said Cribb, 'you'll see that I'm suggesting no such thing. People can be sensitive to other things besides eggs. You'll allow that asthma results from reactions to certain substances and emanations?'

'I can hardly deny it, having written a paper on the subject. Hay, pollen, ipecacuanha, bedfeathers, house-dust. A patient may be affected by any one of these, or something else. My son was sensitive to pollen.'

'Really, sir?' said Cribb. 'Now suppose an asthma patient were discovered to be vulnerable to one of the substances you mention, rather as those Germans were sensitive to egg-white, and someone injected them with a small amount of the substance. What would the result be, do you think?'

'Quite neutral, I should think. The substances affect the breathing, not the blood.'

'Ah, but what if a second injection were given two weeks later?'

'That would be a dangerous thing to try, Sergeant. It might well result in the phenomenon you have described.' Prothero leaned forward across the table, 'But if that was how it happened, you would have found a recent injection-mark on my son's body. There was none—in spite of the inordinately careful examination made by the doctors at the post mortem.'

'That's where my theory foundered,' said Cribb, 'until I took professional advice. I put the case to my Harley Street specialist—hypothetically, of course, with no names mentioned. If a man with the specialised knowledge of substances that cause asthma and similar conditions were to take it into his head to kill another human being, I said, and chose a victim with a known sensitivity to, say, pollen, and a history of asthma, how would he induce the phenomenon known as acute respiratory shock? By grinding the pollen to a fine powder, said my adviser and then taking a very small amount, as little as a tenth of a milligram, and injecting it into the victim, perhaps secreted in some other substance administered in the course of treatment. Then if two weeks later he were suddenly exposed to a slightly larger quantity of the substance, say a milligram, he would die within five minutes. The amounts involved would be so small as to be impossible to detect in a post mortem. Did the second quantity of the substance have to be introduced by means of an injection, I asked? No, said he, certain substances are readily absorbed by skin tissue—nettle leaf irritant, for example, or pollen.'

'This is all very plausible,' said Prothero, 'but when Guy died we were not in a bed of nettles, Sergeant, nor were we coating ourselves with pollen in the hotel garden. So far as I can recollect, there were not even any flowers in the lounge.'

'I established that, sir. Went over everything I could think of until I was ready to give up. Then, as sometimes happens, I was thinking of something quite unconnected with the case, when the very thing I needed to know flashed across my mind. It was the statement the inspector made after I arrived and found you both there with Guy's body. He *told* me the answer, and I was too damned unreceptive to accept it. What were his words, sir?—*"it seemed at first to be the consequence of an over-enthusiastic inhalation of snuff."* That's how you did it, Dr. Prothero. The pollen was in the boy's snuff-box. One inhalation was enough to kill him. You'd mixed it with the snuff that morning knowing Guy wouldn't take any on the ride, but would probably inhale it after lunch.'

'You've had the contents of the snuff-box analysed, I have no doubt,' said Prothero.

'I have, sir, and as you very well know there ain't a microscope invented with sufficient power to detect a quantity of pollen as small as that, nor a chemical test to prove its presence. It's as neat a way of ending a fellow-human's life as I've ever come across. A doctor's way.'

'A father's,' said Prothero, after a pause, 'and not neat, Sergeant.'

'The boy would have killed again if he had lived,' said Cribb. In their context the words were reassuring. For the first time all pretence between the two men had been abandoned. They observed each other with candour, if not respect.

'There is a saying of Hippocrates, the founder of our profession,' said Prothero, '"Extreme remedies are most appropriate for extreme diseases". Believe me when I tell you that I did all I could for Guy while he was alive. At the last, I had to ask myself what future there was for him. I know of other cases, Sergeant, poor wretches with the same dreadful impulse for violence who are kept behind locked doors by devoted parents. Can you imagine what will happen when one of them one day finds a way to slip the latch—for they are intelligent beings as Guy was? The mayhem and the carnage will be beyond belief, Sergeant, striking terror into people's hearts long after the poor demented creature is recaptured by the police or his wretched family. Am I exaggerating?'

'I hope so, sir,' said Cribb quietly. 'I think we'd better move in the direction of the station.'

Prothero raised his eyebrows questioningly. 'Railway—or police?'

'I'd never be able to prove my case in court,' said Cribb with a slight smile. 'Damned lawyers aren't going to get a conviction out of nothing more substantial than an extra week in Brighton . . . Unless you've decided to make a confession. But, as I said, I didn't bring a man with me, or the handcuffs, and it's devilish hard to hear anything anyone says on those confounded trains. I think we've just time to catch that 4.23.'

■ Albert Moscrop finished polishing the latest example of his handiwork, a small, brass telescope with a magnification of four diameters. It represented some three weeks' work, mainly in the evenings, after the shop was closed. He had begun on the day when he had read the newspaper report of the inquest on Bridget. She had been murdered, it had said, by a person or persons unknown, but it was understood that the police had indicated that there was nothing to be gained from further inquiries into the case.

He snapped the telescope shut and placed it on the tissue paper in a narrow wooden box on the table in front of him, making sure that the engraved name 'Jason' was uppermost. Then he closed the box, wrapped it, addressed it and affixed a stamp. As an afterthought, before he took it to the post-office, he turned the parcel over and wrote on the reverse, in small, neat letters, *Eastbourne next year.*